Amish Country

Arson

I0666869

Nurse Hal Among The Amish Series

Book 8

Fay Risner

Copyright (c) 2015
All Rights Reserved
Fay Risner

ISBN 13 9780982459584

ISBN 10 0982459580

Booksbyfay Publisher
Author, Editor and Publisher Fay Risner
fayrisner@netins.net

Fay Risner's books
Nurse Hal Among The Amish Series

A Promise Is A Promise   Doubting Thomas
The Rainbow's End   Amish Country Arson
Hal's Worldly Temptations
As Her Name Is So Is Redbird
Emma's Gossamer Dreams
The Courting Buggy

Amazing Gracie Historical Mystery Series

Neighbor Watchers   Poor Defenseless Addie
Specious Nephew   Will O Wisp
The Country Seat Killer
The Chance Of A Sparrow
Moser Mansion Ghosts
Locked Rock, Iowa Hatchet Murders

Westerns
Stringbean Hooper Westerns   Tread Lightly Sibby
The Dark Wind Howls Over Mary   The Blue Bonnet-novella
Small Feet's Many Moon Journey   A Coffin To Lie On-novella
Ella Mayfield's Pawpaw Militia-Civil War

Mystery
The Answering Machine Knew
Christmas books
Christmas Traditions - An Amish Love Story   Christmas With Hover Hill
Leona's Christmas Bucket List
Fiction

Listen To Me Honey – novella
Robot Grandma - novella

Children Books
Spooks In Claiborne Mansion   My Children Are More Precious Than Gold
Mr. Quacker

Nonfiction about Alzheimer's disease

Open A Window - Caregiver Handbook
Hello Alzheimer's Goodbye Dad-author's true story

Cookbook
Midwest Favorite Lamb Recipes
Books published by Booksbyfay Publisher
Romance
Sunset Til Sunrise On Buttercup Lane by Connie Risner

Military-nonfiction-Vietnam War
Redcatcher MP by Mickey Bright

3

Love Your Enemies

But I say unto you, Love your enemies, bless them that curse you, do good to them that hate you, and pray for them which despitefully use you, and persecute you;

Matthew 5:44

Chapter 1

A golden draft horse, with a white mane, tramped on the hard country road. The resounding thuds feathered the long, white hairs on his hooves, vibrated up the work horse's legs and through the rider's body. Amish riders were used to squeezing their legs into a horse's stomach to stay on when they rode bareback. This ride wasn't anything new for the skilled rider on this horse's back.

This night near the end of September was dark, pitch dark. The rider purposely planned the excursion for such a night. Darkness was good for what was about to happen.

The hour was midnight. Amish farmers were in bed, asleep until their alarm clocks went off at four in the morning. That's when they started their day in the barn, milking their cows.

The buildings in the dark shadows off to the right of the horse were John Lapp's farm.

I was told John Lapp is married to an English redhead who calls herself a nurse. If that woman, with a man's name, becomes a bother, she and her family will be next to be punished by me.

In the still of night, the horse's tromps sounded like someone beating a drum. It wouldn't be good if the Lapp dog raced to the road to bark at the horse. That mutt would alert the Lapps someone was traveling on the road at a late hour.

The rider relaxed. *Gute! The horse is past the Lapp farm with no problems from the dog. Next farm coming up belongs to the old bishop and his wife, Elton and Jane Bontrager. They seemed to be kindly people. Even if they were not, it would not do to ever bother them. The Amish community would not stand for retaliation against their bishop.*

The horse trotted through the crossroads. Suddenly, the Stolfus cornfield was near. The dark shapes of corn shocks and silhouette of corn plants stood out against the night time sky. Harvest was under way in the Amish community but not near finished. With a tug on the reins, the horse slowed. A pull on the right rein made the horse turned into the cornfield driveway. The rider stayed in the grass along the fence and headed toward the back barn yard fence.

Soon Chicken Plucker Jonah Stolfus and his family will be in for a rude awakening. I heard what he did to that young girl. Shot her in the head he did. He killed her and her with a baby to raise. He got away with that cruelty until now. No one should feel sorry enough to help a man that would do anything that mean.

Work horses, carriage horses and milk cows milled together in the barn yard. Restless stock came out of the barn while others entered. The rider slowed the horse to a walk. One of the horses nickered a greeting. The draft horse lifted his head, threw back his ears and neighed back. The rider patted the horse's neck to silence him.

I do not want the stock riled up by my strange horse. That could get me run over. "Whoa. Jack." *I will tie to a fence post so I can slide off on the other side of the fence. It will be easier to climb down the boards and back up to mount this tall horse.*

The rider stuck a leg over the board, searching for footing in the cattle panel.

Ouch! The barbed wire along the top of the fence stuck my

2

leg. When I come back, I need to remember to swing my leg wider so I miss the barbs.

Now walk slowly to the barn. The horses see me. They have bunched up in the corner, snorting and stomping their hooves at me. Some of the cattle are lined up in the opposite corner, watching suspiciously while others ran into the barn to hide from me. That is gute. Gives me more space to work.

The animals are sniffing the breeze. They cannot recognize my scent. They are not used to a stranger among them this time of night.

It is too dark to see where I put my feet, but that is gute. I need the cover of darkness for this job. I will just have to be careful not to stub my toes on the unleveled, hoof pocked ground. I cannot afford to fall. I might get trampled if the horses and cattle bolt.

A moment was taken to make a quick survey of the house from beside the barn. The windows remained unlit as every other house along the road had been. The far corner of the barn was partially hidden from the house.

This is the spot. I am out of sight here. I will kneel and empty my jacket pockets so I can make short work of this job.

A small, plastic juice bottle of kerosene and two scrap rags dropped to the ground. The other pocket bulged with matches. Fingers circled around one wooden match stem.

It is always so easy to start a fire. Why not? I am an expert at this now.

Thumb pressure popped the cap off the juice bottle. The stringent smell of kerosene caused the rider's nose to wrinkle.

Drizzle the kerosene down the side of the barn and watch the run off soak into the rags. Now scratch the match head over a nail.

A search in the dark by running finger tips over the barn boards found the rusty edge of a nail head. The match hissed and flared into flame.

I need to stand up and at arm's length before I throw the match on the rags so I do not get burned.

The burning match landed in the middle of the rags. The

flame brightened by kerosene grew larger as it spread. Whoosh! The rags exploded. The flames flared, licking up the kerosene soaked barn boards.

Almost too close to stand yet. I must remember how far back to stand when I throw the next match.

A nervous peek around the barn corner found the house still dark, but it wouldn't be for long.

I am standing in a lit area now. This is not gute. Listening to the racket the livestock is making has me nervous.

The Stolfus horses panicked at the sight of fire. They whinnied and bucked when they heard the crackling noises and smelled the flames. The cows bellowed and coughed as puffs of smoke surrounded them.

I've got to get out of here before the household wakes up.

The figure ran to the fence post where the draft horse waited and clambered up the boards. Sensing danger, the Stolfus horses skittered, bucking this way and that. They wanted out of the pen in the worst way. They bunched together for safety and stampeded in a circle along the fence headed toward the fence climber.

The arsonist was almost safe. With one leg over the fence and sliding along the draft horse's broad back and inching down the horse's far side.

Before the rider's other leg was safely out of the way, the rushing horses hugged the fence. The nearest horse pinned the rider's outstretched leg and foot to the board. The foot turned sideways stressing the ankle the wrong way and causing the grating snap of the ankle bone. The horse's weight pushed against the leg, rubbing it along the barbed wire. The barbs bit into the calf flesh and ripped a furrow from the knee to the ankle. The arsonist's anguished cry resulted from the sensation of horrific leg pain. Agony brought on a sick stomach, whirling eyesight and then dimmed vision. In an instant, the herd of horses had raced past, and the leg came free from the wire.

I've got to get out of here. My scream surely was heard above the ruckus of the livestock. I feel like I might have a black out spell. If I did, I would fall off Jack. I better be far

4

away from here if that happens.

The obedient draft horse had shied at the rider's scream. Once the reins were unwrapped from the top board, it took a second for the rider to calm the skittish horse. Jack smelled the smoke and heard the ruckus the frightened livestock in the barn yard made. He shuddered as his senses told him he was in as much danger as the other livestock.

The increasing night breeze cooled the rider's body of its feverish heat and made it easier to think.

I have to let my leg dangle no matter how much it hurts. I cannot think about the throbbing pain in my leg and ankle. I have to get away quickly.

The rider rubbed the thigh of the injured leg and made teeth gritting sounds as the action didn't help the discomfort.

Given his head, Jack trotted in the grassy strip back to the road as if he knew where he had to go. The rider stopped, used both hands to grip the injured leg and shifted on the horse's back. Just a quick glance back to see what had happened so far. The blazing barn lit up the other building sites. Horses and cows milled frantically in the lighted heat. Some still rubbed the fences to find a way out of the pen. The din of noise added to the animals panic.

Disappointment went through the rider regarding the leg injury. What bad luck that the accident prevented a closer viewing of the fire. A surge of relief followed. In the darkness, no one could make out the rider and horse this far away from the Stolfus barn.

Dashing hopes of a successful burn came with the sight of someone already in the barn yard, opening the back gate to free the livestock into the cornfield. How was it possible the fire had been noticed so fast before more than one side of the barn was aflame?

The disgusted rider laid down on the horse's broad neck. "Go, Jack. Nothing more that I can do here. Run for home."

The ride back home wasn't going to be nearly as enjoyable as the journey to the Stolfus farm. The leg pain was greater and becoming more unbearable with each hard step of the horse's hooves. Passing the Bontrager and Lapp farms, the rider uttered soft groans, hugging tightly to the horse's neck.

The rider slowed Jack and straightened up to check out the landmarks. On the highway south of Wickenburg, the red and blue lights of fire engines whirled against the dark sky. No sound of sirens yet from that far away, but the fire equipment sped with urgency toward the country road. The bitter taste of poor timing formed in the rider's mouth.

Help is coming much too quickly. That is too bad. A phone shed must be close to the Stolfus farm. The barn would have burnt to the ground before the fire trucks arrived if more time had gone by. Next time I'll torch the phone shed first.

The black shape of uneven tree tops stood out against the sky. Bender Creek dirt road turn off was coming up. The peepers and crickets were singing up a storm. Across the road along the banks of Bender Creek, bull frogs competed to see which one could croak the loudest. In the distance, the sudden high pitched yap of coyotes on the run made Jack shudder. It took a gentle hand rubbing his neck to quiet him.

Here is my turn off. I will get behind the tree line in the clearing where I can hide. There I can rest a minute. It is fun to watch the parade of fire trucks going so fast. I hear the sirens now. What a joyful sound!

In an instant, four fire trucks and an ambulance sped by and were quickly out of the arsonist's view. For only a moment, the area was a kaleidoscope of swirling reds and blues. Now all that remained was the fading sirens. The timber had become silent. The peepers and frogs music ceased while they tried to figure out if the reverberating noises they heard was dangerous to them.

Might as well go home. With the way my leg hurts, I will not walk much for a few days. I need to get off this horse and into bed. The rider nudged the horse with the good knee. "Go, Jack. Pick your way through the timber back the way we came."

Jonah Stolfus woke with a start to find his bedroom illuminated by an eerie, orange glow flickering up and down the walls. He heard the panicked cries of his livestock and feared the worst before he knew for sure what happened.

Jonah jumped up and ran to the window. Horrified, he saw the south side of his barn in flames. In the light from the fire, he spotted the dark forms of a horse and rider racing for the cornfield gate hole. At the moment, he didn't have time to wonder why anyone would be in his cornfield at the same time his barn was burning. He had more pressing worries.

"Freda, get up," Jonah said, heading for his clothes.

His wife sat up in bed, wondering at Jonah's frenzied actions. "Was ist letz?"

Jonah yanked on his trousers and pulled his galluses over his nightshirt. "Hurry! Get the children up and out of the house. The barn is on fire.

As close as the barn is, it might cause the house to burn. I see sparks flying this direction, carried by the wind. Get the children as far away as you can to be safe. Tell Stanley to go to the phone shed as fast as he can run to call the fire department. Send Jason and Davie to help me get the livestock out of the pen."

In the next moment, Jonah entered the barn yard and darted in a zig zag out of the frightened animals way as he headed to the back gate. He opened the gate and called.

The cattle and horses, blinded by the brilliant glow of the blaze, smoke and heat, milled into each other. Jonah edged around the fence to get behind them and joined his boys. Jason, eleven years old, and Davie, ten, spread out, waving their arms and clapping their hands.

As fire shot up inside the barn, two horses bolted out the door and nearly ran over Davie. He hadn't been able to move fast since a riding accident broke his left leg and left him with a limp.

One horse stumbled out of the barn and fell over dead. Jonah's stomach did a sickening roll when he saw the tortured animal torched by the fire. The bull staggered out the barn door. He appeared to be blind, badly burned and shivering.

The livestock rushed away from Jonah. The boys yelled as

7

loud as they could and waved their hands. The bull followed along with them. Finally, the cows and horses found the open gate hole and spread across the field to cool safety.

"Should we check in the barn?" Jason yelled at his father to be heard above the roaring blaze.

"Nah, it is too dangerous." Jonah sucked in smoke. He had a coughing fit and took his blue work handkerchief out of his pocket to cover his nose to filter the air. "Let's get away from the smoke."

Jason and Davie walked out around the horse carcass. With tears in his eyes, Jason lamented, "Poor Slow Poke got roasted alive."

High pitched warbles brought John Lapp sat straight up in bed. Red and blue lights circled the room, bouncing from one wall to another. His heart raced as he leaped out of bed and ran to the window.

Hal put her feet on the floor and lit the lamp. "John, was ist letz?"

John ran his fingers through his dark brown hair as he stared at the darkness. "There is a fire somewhere, but not here. The fire trucks are going by Elton Bontrager's farm now."

From downstairs, Aunt Tootie yelled shrilly, "Fire! Fire! The fire trucks are coming. Get out quickly. The house is on fire."

Nora Lindstrom grumbled as she padded past Hal and John's bedroom door on bare feet. "I better get downstairs and calm Tootie down."

Noah and Daniel's low voices chattered in their room. Wide eyed, Redbird and Beth stood up, rubbed the sleep from their eyes and peered over the baby crib at their parents. Hal went to the crib to reassure them. "Can you see a fire, John?"

"Jah, a big one. Looks like it is at Chicken Plucker Jonah's farm. I can't tell which building is burning, but the blaze is high in the air. The fire trucks are just about there now." John turned to Hal with worry in his dark brown eyes. "I'm getting dressed and go see if I can help."

"Wonder what time it is?" Hal walked back to the bedside table, and focused the lamp light on the alarm clock. "One thirty in the morning. I should go along. There might be need of a nurse. Should the boys go with us?"

"Nah, they can stay here and milk if we are still gone by chore time," John answered back as he shoved his shirt tail in his trousers. He left to hitch up the buggy.

Hal dressed and pulled her prayer cap over her frizzy red hair. Out in the hall, Noah, eighteen years old, and Daniel, sixteen, leaned against the wall. Hal's father, Jim, stood beside them. Hal paused long enough to tell the boys they could milk if they didn't make it home in time.

Jim offered to help the boys. With a yawn, he told Noah and Daniel, if he couldn't do anything else he was going back to bed, and they should, too.

Hal stopped in the clinic to see about Aunt Tootie. Her night cap was crooked and gray curls spilled out around it. She sat up the bed, clutching a hand full of her light blue cotton night gown as she breathed heavily. Hal's mother, Nora, sat beside the elderly woman, propping her up. When Hal looked troubled, Nora rolled her eyes toward the ceiling.

"Are you all right, Aunt Tootie?" Hal asked.

Aunt Tootie patted her chest and took a deep breath. "I'm having a spell of the vapors, but I'm calmer now that I know the fire isn't here."

"Gute for you. The fire's a couple miles away at the Stolfus farm. John and I are going to see if there's anything we can do to help," Hal told them. "Mom, I settled the girls down. You might check on them when you go back to bed. Dad says he isn't getting back up until milk time. The girls will want out of bed when they know you're up for the day."

Just passed the intersection, a fire pickup parked cross way on the road. The fireman, in the middle of the road, stopped John's buggy. "You can't come pass here."

"Would it be all recht if we left the buggy in the corn field and walked in? My wife is Nurse Hal. We wondered if there was anything we can do to help our neighbors." John explained.

"The ambulance came with us, but you and Nurse Hal are welcome to walk in if you want to see if the family is all right. I stopped here so I don't know what the circumstances are except the barn is on fire," the fireman said.

Four fire trucks surrounded the blazing barn as sprays of water arched into the hissing flames, creating huge plumes of black smoke. The ambulance parked along the edge of the driveway. The three paramedics, Daryl, Steve and Ivan, leaned against the front of the ambulance, watching the action.

Daryl looked around to see who was coming. "Look who is here, fellows. Hello, Nurse Hal."

"Hello. I see you're working hard," Hal said, smiling at them.

"We're hoping we don't have to this trip," Steve replied.

"Amen to that," Hal declared as she walked toward Jonah Stolfus's family. Freda and the children gathered at the far end of the front yard as close to the country road that headed north as they could get. Hal walked across the yard toward white forms barely visible in the hazy smoke. The children left the house in their nightshirts with only a blanket around their shoulders to ward off the night chill. Freda had managed to slip on a dress. Her white nightgown was visible below the navy blue dress hem.

Standing beside the family was a neighbor, Rosemary Nisely. "Wilcom, Hal, I am so glad you came. Your comfort is needed." She nodded toward Freda.

Hal put her arms around Freda and gave the woman a hug. "I'm so sorry this happened."

"Jonah told me to get the children out of the house and far away. He said the barn might spark the house on fire since it is so close. Praise God, the fire trucks came so fast. They wet the house down and saved it," Freda said, swiping a curl out of her eyes with a trembling hand and stuffing it under her prayer cap where it belonged.

"You and your family are all safe which is a gute thing,"

Roseanna said to comfort her.

"Jah, the barn can be replaced," Hal assured.

Freda kept her eyes on the inferno. "It is such a frightening, terrifying experience to have a fire break out so close when we were all asleep." She raised her eyes to the star studded sky. "It is God's will that Jonah woke up in time to save us all. Praise the Lord!"

"Amen," Hal and Roseanna said together.

John joined Chicken Plucker Jonah, his three teenage boys and neighbors, Samuel Nisely and Eli Miller, in time to watch the barn's roof topple into the blaze. The thunderous crash seared through the hearts and souls of the men. With a sinking feeling, Chicken Plucker's neighbors were thinking it could just as easily have been their barn.

"Our house is too close to the burning barn. Look behind you. The home's vinyl siding buckled from the heat of the flames. If the fire company had arrived ten minutes later, my house would have caught fire. The men wet the house down to cool it off," Chicken Plucker explained, nervously stroking his dark beard.

"The siding can be replaced. Praise the Lord, your home did not burn down, and your family is safe," John reasoned. His sympathetic eyes met the woeful blue ones of fair haired Samuel and the dark, empathetic ones of young Eli. They both nodded their heads in agreement.

Jonah's mind tumbled with worries as he rambled on. "You should see my livestock. The hair is burnt off most of them. It wonders me how many I might lose. Slow Poke is dead. Roasted alive he was. A cow died, and the bull was having trouble staying on his feet to go into the cornfield.

How do we manage milking after this? It is not going to be easy to milk forty head of cows out in the open twice a day."

"My barn is empty. You can use it to house your milk cows," Samuel said. "We will run the cattle and horses down the road to my barn. You will not have far to come to milk."

"I can help round the stock up after daylight," Eli offered.

The volunteer chief of the Wickenburg fire department, Charlie Miller, a chunky man in his fifties, sauntered toward them. "Mr. Stolfus, we're getting the fire under control now that the barn collapsed. It may be after daybreak yet before we leave. All that hay in the barn will smolder for a long time. We want to make sure it doesn't flare back up. Wind's supposed to be strong from the east today. We're still worried for your house."

"Denki to you, and the other firemen for your hard work." Another weary thought crossed his mind as he's eyes met John's. "That was my whole winter supply of hay gone up in smoke. What a waste!"

John put a hand on the distraught man's shoulder. "I have extra bales I can give you."

"So do I," Samuel said. "We can get plenty of hay from others to fill a new barn."

"I know one thing. With God's will, if I have a new barn, it will be built a lot farther away from the house," Jonah declared.

"I have to ask you a few questions," Fire Chief Miller said. "Do you have any idea how the fire started? Did you leave a lit lantern in the barn?"

Jonah shook his head. "Nah, we bring all the lanterns to the house with us. As short as the days are, it is night when we come to the house. Still dark when we go back to the barn in the morning to milk so we need the lanterns to see where we are walking."

"Did you have any inflammable liquids stored in the barn?"

"Nah," Chicken Plucker Jonah answered.

"After daylight, I need to look around to see what could have caused a fire in a hundred year old barn that doesn't have electric wires running to it," the fire chief said.

"When I first looked out the window at the fire, I saw a horse leaving the cornfield gate hole and head east on the road. I think there was a person on the horse, but I cannot be sure. It was so dark," Jonah said.

"If this is a case of suspected arson, I have to call Sheriff Dawson. He'll investigate with me." Chief Miller added irritably, "We need to catch the person and punish him for this horrible act."

Jonah gave the man a kindly look. "Denki, but we should not be so harsh or act too quickly. I stood here watching my barn burn and wondered why such a thing happened to me.

I do not harbor an angry or bitter thought. All I feel is a huge sense of loss." As he watched the fire die out, he made a decision and spoke. "I hope if someone did set the fire, with the help of God, he will feel the hand of God directing him to change his ways. He will become remorseful for his harmful deed and convert himself."

Fire Chief Miller shook his head, disagreeing. "It has been my experience it doesn't work that way. If someone lit that fire on purpose, don't expect the man to change. That never happens, because an arsonist is a sick person. I know. I've put out many a fire caused by people who get a thrill out of setting the fire." He paused, then added, "Usually, they stick around to watch the building burn as long as they can without getting caught. That sounds like what the fellow on the horse did. He watched from the cornfield until he saw your bedroom light come on, Jonah."

Chapter 2

When John and Hal returned home, dawn was just slipping a layer of red over the eastern horizon. As John parked the buggy by the barn, Biscuit, the boy's cream colored coon hound, rose from in front of the barn. He raced to greet the buggy with his yapping bark. John parked by the barn, and Biscuit peed on a back wheel.

The generator was humming yet so John headed for the barn.

Jim greeted, "We're just about done."

John said, "You must have gotten an early start this morning."

Jim shook his head yes. "None of us could go back to sleep for worrying about the Stolfus family. We spent some time looking out the west windows at the flames. That wasn't doing any good so the boys and I figured it was time to milk."

Hal found her mother, Nora, and Aunt Tootie preparing breakfast. Redbird and Beth, in their high chairs, chattered and kicked their bare feet excitedly when they saw their mother. She bent to give them each a kiss on the cheek.

"I should start the laundry while I still have some energy left. I'll get the wash water heated and put a load of clothes in the washing machine," Hal said.

"What was burning?" Aunt Tootie asked.

"The barn," Hal said wearily.

"Is the fire out now?" Nora asked.

Hal shook her head no. "Not quite. The firemen are staying as long as it takes to spray the smoldering hay that was in the loft. They're afraid the strong breeze will carry sparks toward the house."

"Was anyone hurt?" Aunt Tootie asked as she flipped the sizzling sausage cakes in the iron skillet.

"Nah, the family woke up in time to get outside. This will be a costly fire for the family with loss of livestock and hay. I'm sure the cows milk production will cut way down while they aren't feeling well. A lot of them were burnt and may died. The horses might be sick, too. Watching their livestock suffer is an awful time for the Stolfus family," lamented Hal.

Just before breakfast, Hal carried a wicker basket of clothes through the wet grass to the clothes line. A light frost had glazed everything earlier, but the blaring sun melted it to glittering beads of cold dew.

Damp bits of fresh mowed grass clung to her bare feet. Hal stood on one foot and rubbed it with the other then reversed the procedure to remove the pieces of grass. The generator was quiet in the barn. The men must be finished.

Daniel had opened the chicken house door on the way to milk. Tom Turkey joined his harem of hens, scratching in the barn yard. Funny how Tom realized Abraham, the rooster, wasn't around anymore. He saw his chance to became ruler of the chicken flock.

That reminded Hal that she had to go with John soon to the salebarn. She needed to buy her own rooster if she wanted to hatch chicks next spring for fryers and pullets. Emma took Abraham and half the flock of hens to her new home when she married Adam.

What would happen when the new rooster tried to take over the hens? Hal was afraid Tom wasn't going to like giving up his senior position. When Tom Turkey didn't like something he had quite a temper.

Near the lean-to, Buttercat had a successful hunt going on

in a game of cat and mouse. He threw a mouse up in the air and sent it a few feet from him. Once the mouse landed and crawled away, Buttercat pounced under the courting buggy after it.

Hal grimaced as she watched the weak mouse belly along the ground. It was all right for the cat to play with the nasty thing as long as he kept it near the barn. If the mouse got away, which was doubtful, it would hopefully escape to the barn instead of coming to the house.

Biscuit flattened in the grass by the barn door with one ear alert, waiting for the boys to come out. He'd sprint to life quick enough with his tail whipping and follow them as soon as they appeared.

The happy wren in the maple tree chortled a loud serenade. Weary as she was, Hal didn't appreciate the noise this morning. She picked a shirt out of the basket and shook it at the tree, shouting, "Hush, Wren! Go away."

The wet, blue shirt made a popping sound as it straightened out. The wren quit singing long enough to climb higher in the tree. As soon as he felt safe, he started his chortles again.

Hal shaded her eyes with her hand and searched out the tiny bird, one of God's happy creatures. As she stuck a clothes pin on the shirt tail, she instantly felt guilty. She shouldn't take her bad mood out on that little bird. He had given her hours of pleasure. "All recht, I'm sorry, Mr. Wren. Sing your heart out for me, but could you keep the volume down? You didn't lose sleep last night like I did."

Hal picked up the empty basket and noticed the men and boys, peeking over the barn door, smothering laughter. Hal headed to the back door as she yelled over her shoulder. "Breakfast is ready."

After breakfast, Hal carried the last load of clothes to the line. At the sound of slowing clip clops, her attention focused on the buggy turning into the driveway. Bishop Elton Bontrager pulled to a stop by the house yard. His wife, Jane, and he climbed down.

"Wilcom, Elton. The men are in the barn. They left the clean up until after breakfast. They should be almost done," Hal called.

The short, rolly poly man waved over his shoulder as he walked to the barn. The bishop acted like a man on a mission. His wife walked across the yard toward Hal. Jane's hair had more gray in the brown every time Hal saw her. "Gute Morgen, Sister Jane. You're up and going early."

Jane looked solemn."We had excitement in the neighborhood last night, ain't so? Elton and I could not sleep after the fire trucks woke us up for worrying about the Stolfus family."

Hal brought a pair of trousers from the basket and shook them out. "Jah, how scary that was when the fire trucks went by in the night. The frightful noise woke everyone. Scared the girls and Aunt Tootie worse than the rest of us. Honestly, sometimes she's harder to calm down than Redbird and Beth."

"Even scarier yet is the fact someone deliberately set that fire." Jane picked up a smaller pair of trousers and stuck her hand in the clothes pin bag as she shook the trousers one handed. "We just came from the Stolfus farm. Jonah sure was missing his barn this morning at milking time. The cows are skittish, and they did not want to cooperate out in the open."

"I can imagine. His cows are used to a milking machine just like ours. Hand milking seemed strange to them."

"Fortunately, between Jonah, his boys, Eli Mast and Samuel Nisely they moved the cows down the road to Samuel's barn. Samuel and Eli were going to helped finish the milking."

"Jane, you don't have to help with this," Hal protested half heartedly.

"You had a short night already with lots more work ahead of you than I will have to do today." Jane turned and waved at the men as they walked up the porch steps and went in the house.

The dog was trailing along behind the boys. He stopped at the steps, made three turns in the grass and curled up to sleep. He'd patiently wait for the boys to come outside.

Jane said, "Sure enough, I will help you finish recht quick. As soon as we are done, we can join the men and have a cup of coffee.

We watched the fire trucks out the window in the night and saw John and you go by. Recht after you left for home, we drove to the Stolfus farm to see if anyone was hurt. We prayed with Jonah and his family and the men helping them. So you see our night was short, too."

"Sure enough. We'll need a cup of coffee or two to keep us going this day. When I think of the daily needs for this family, I am so thankful Mom and Aunt Tootie are still here. They're such a help to me. This morning, they cooked breakfast. John and I got home just in time to help them eat it, and that left me time to do the laundry. Now that the days cool off fast if I don't get the clothes on the line early, they don't have time to dry.

Dad helped the boys the milk. I sure am going to miss my parents and Aunt Tootie when they go home," Hal confessed. "Especially, when I have to do all the cooking again."

"Maybe they will not leave for a while yet. Do not worry until it is time to worry," Jane suggested, patting Hal's shoulder.

"It's time recht now to worry. Dad is already making hints about leaving for home soon before the snow flies. I can't blame him. I don't want him to have to drive on slick roads," Hal said woefully, fastening the last pair of trousers with a clothes pin.

"You should have more faith in yourself, Hal Lapp. You will do fine without any help. I am sure of it. You managed alone while Emma taught school all day," encouraged Jane.

Hal put the empty basket on her hip. "Emma left me a list each morning of tasks to do and suggestions for meals. When she came home, she corrected the mistakes I made or worked fast to finish what I didn't get done."

"There is a world of difference between that girl and you. Emma is speedy and experienced homemaker. You have yet to learn and do the tasks at your own speed. You can do it," Jane bolstered.

18

As they headed back to the porch, Hal stopped. "Ach, nah. Look at my pretty marigolds, will you?"

Jane's face scrunched up in dislike as she studied the mashed plants' dirty yellow flowers. "How did they get in such an awful shape?"

Hal moved closer. "Something dug here. See how the flowers are covered with dirt."

"Must have been the dog," Jane surmised.

"Biscuit has never done this before in my flower beds," Hal defended.

"Still when a dog has a bone to bury he usually picks the softest dirt to dig the hole," Jane said knowingly.

Hal marched up the steps. "Let's go see what the boys have to say about this."

Swinging their legs back and forth to hear their feet slap against the high chair legs, the two years old little girls were impatient. Redbird, a redhead, looked very much like her mother. Beth, with light brown hair, resembled her late mother, Anna. The toddlers were restless. They would rather be on the floor, free to wander around. The front door banged shut. They twisted in their high chairs at the sound of familiar men's voices in the living room. When the men entered the kitchen, Redbird saw Elton among them. She gave him a wide smile as she held her hands out to him, begging for him to set her free.

Elton looked at John for permission. "Will it be all recht if I hold Redbird?"

"Sure enough. I better warn you after the girls have rutsched around this might be Redbird's way to get to the floor. She might not let you hold her long, " John advised, releasing the tray from the chair.

Elton grinned at him. "I will take my changes."

When Beth saw Redbird get her freedom, she held her arms up to Jim with a begging look on her face. "I'd say my buddy wants out of her chair, too." He took off the tray and rescued Beth.

As soon as the men were seated, Aunt Tootie came around

19

with coffee cups and the pot.

Elton blew on his steaming cup and took a small sip before he set the cup down. "John, I just came from the Stolfus farm. We need to organize a barn raising as soon as possible. Jonah needs a barn set up for milking. It will not be as handy going to Samuel Nisely's to milk by hand with as many cows as he has. Jonah will be over there several times a day with plenty of vet work to do on the burnt stock, too. That all takes time and is unhandy."

"You announce that at the worship service this Sunday during the member meeting. We will get organized recht away," John agreed.

Jim set his cup down. "Did Mr. Stolfus figure out what caused the fire?"

"The sheriff arrived to investigate before we left," Elton said. "Jonah saw someone on horse back leaving his cornfield. The rider headed east. It was too dark to make out more than that when he looked out the bedroom window. The sheriff thinks someone set the fire."

"That's awful," Aunt Tootie said, hanging her dish towel on the line behind the cookstove. "What is this world coming to when someone can be that mean for no reason?"

"Why would anyone burn that man's nice big barn," Nora declared on her way out the back door to empty the dish pan.

Elton picked up his cup and took a drink while he pondered his answer. He set the cup down to respond. "We may never know what makes a man do such an evil act, but this is the only world we have. It is filled with all kinds of people, gute and bad.

Jonah looked out the window in time to see the fire started on the southeast side of the barn. The sheriff and fire chief looked there first. They found a fragment of a plastic juice bottle and a white lid. Partial label looked like it might be a ten ounce Tropicana Orange Juice. The plastic smelled of kerosene.

Sheriff Dawson wanted the names of boys in rumspringa. He wondered if they had been joy riding and drinking. One of them might have torched the barn for a prank."

"Did you come up with names?" John asked.

"I gave him a few in strict confidence, but I did not want to accuse anyone. I explained to the sheriff our teenagers are allowed rumspringa, before they commit to our faith. Sometimes, they act more English than Plain. That does not make them guilty of such a horrible crime. Noah and Daniel, you know the boys I am thinking of. Have you heard one of them brag they were about to set a fire?" The bishop asked.

Noah looked at Daniel, and Daniel shook his head no. "We have not. If we had, we would have told Daed."

"Gute," Elton Bontrager said. "If you ever hear anything let your father know. Such a deed by a young person would be cause for bragging, especially by one that is drinking. Others would know about this. We do not want more fires. If Jonah had not woke up when he did, the house would have caught fire. Some of their family may have perished. We hear of that happening all the time."

Daniel said, "There is a party in the timber on Bender Creek road a week from Friday night. That is the place such bragging might happen."

The bishop perked up. "Would you boys be willing to go to this party and listen to the talk?" He glanced at John and saw his frown. "Of course, that is if your father is willing to let you."

"Noah and Daniel stay away from such parties. They are level headed. I am proud of them for knowing their faith and family are more important than joining in evil English ways. I think getting involved with a group that has one or more arsonists is dangerous," John stated.

"What if Daniel and I took Biscuit for a practice run Friday night before we start coon hunting?" We could use that for an excuse. We just happened to walk in on the party and hang out for a while," Noah said.

All at the table watched John as he wrestled with his decision. "Sure enough, I think this could be dangerous. Against my better judgment, if you do not stay long and will be very careful to not let on why you are really at the party I will say jah."

Elton stared into his cup. His head jerked back, and he narrowed his eyes at Redbird. She grinned at him and clapped her hands.

"Was ist letz, Elton?" John asked.

"I am ferhoodled. My coffee cup is empty, and I know I did not drink all of it," Elton said, grinning at Redbird.

"Redbird, shame on you," Daniel scolded.

Redbird stuck her tongue out at Daniel and leaned back against Elton for protection from her brother. That caused everyone to laugh.

"What's so funny" Hal asked as she entered the kitchen with Jane right behind her.

"Elton has a mystery. His cup went dry, and he did not empty the cup himself." John chuckled as he pointed at Redbird.

"Well, the rest of you won't find it so funny when you're the one holding that child. She does that to me all the time. Dad, you better check your cup. Beth copies whatever her sister does. She may have drank yours dry," Hal warned.

Beth had Jim's cup to her mouth. He took it from her and looked in the cup. "I rescued a swallow or two." Jim smiled at her as he teased, "You get your own cup, girl."

Beth pouted and held her hands out to take the cup. "Mine, mine."

"Aunt Tootie, could you please bring us more coffee." Hal tossed the basket in the mud room, before she sit next to Elton. "Get a cup of milk for Redbird and Beth so they won't bother the coffee cups, and you two join us. You need to take a break, too."

Elton mentioned, "Have you heard there is a new family bought the farm next to Moses and Stella Strutt?"

"What happened to Amos Boxholder?" John asked.

"He moved into a grossdawdi house William built for him by his house. William cannot handle farming both farms so they had to sell Amos's farm," Elton explained. "Jane and I visited with the new couple yesterday. I wanted to give them directions to next Sunday's service at Luke Yoder's farm.

"How many in the family?" Hal asked.

"Enoch Bruner and his wife, Wanda, and the wife's sister, Gladys Kraybill. The sister lives in the old grossdawdi house next to the house that belonged to Amos's parents years ago. We did not see her. Wanda Bruner said she was not feeling well," Elton said.

"I'll introduce myself to them on Sunday so they know where to come if they need medical help," Hal said. She focused on Noah and Daniel across from her. "Have you seen the mess your dog made of my flowers at the end of the porch? I know it's about time to pull them and clean the bed, but I wanted to enjoy the flowers as long as I could before they froze."

Noah looked puzzled. "Was ist letz with the flowers?"

"Biscuit uprooted some of them. The rest he covered with dirt and mashed the plants over," Hal said testily. "Go see for yourselves."

The boys headed for the door, and they weren't gone long. Noah declared, "Biscuit did not do that digging."

"How do you know that?" Jane asked.

"Whatever dug was clearing a hole so it could go under the porch to hide," Daniel said.

"What kind of animal does that?" Aunt Tootie's hand went to her throat. "That end of the porch is close to where I sleep."

Noah shrugged. "We do not know yet. We filled in the hole. Maybe the animal is gone."

The next morning after kitchen cleanup, Hal said, "I'm going to rake leaves off the yard and garden into the road ditch to burn."

"Looks like a nice morning to do yard work." Nora turned to Aunt Tootie. "You want to watch the girls or help Hal rake leaves."

Aunt Tootie said quickly, "I can watch the girls and start

lunch if you aren't done by then."

Nora winked at Hal. "That's fine, Tootie. Hal, find me a rake."

Hal and Nora made the trip to the tool shed. As they walked by the end of the porch, Hal glanced at her flower bed. Her marigolds were buried under another pile of dirt. A gaping hole tunneled under the porch.

"Oh no, look, Mom. That critter didn't leave. We need to do something to run him off," Hal declared. "I'll ask Dad and John what they think we should do when they get back from town."

The women managed to clean the yard in time to start lunch. As Hal put Nora's rake in the tool shed, she said, "I don't know how long the men will be gone to Wickenburg after supplies. We won't wait lunch on them. They can eat when they get back."

They were climbing the porch steps when Nora reached out and took Hal by the arm to stop her. She grinned. "How about we sit for a few minutes to rest? Tootie said she could start lunch. Let's hold her to it once."

"Sure enough, I'm for that. I'm bushed," Hal agreed as they sat on the porch swing.

When Hal finally felt guilty enough to check on her aunt, Aunt Tootie was bustling around in the kitchen, preparing the meal. She chattered to the girls, seated on the floor. They quietly watched her pace back and forth and listened as if they knew what she was telling them about each recipe.

By the time, lunch was ready, the men and boys were home. First thing on Hal's mind after the noon prayer was the animal under the porch. "That animal was digging again last night. We've got to figure out a way to stop it from destroying my flower bed. What can we do?"

"We have a coon trap you could use," Noah suggested.

"Gute, rig it up and see if the animal will go in it," Hal said.

Daniel grinned at her. "It is probably a skunk. I caught a faint whiff of skunk odor yesterday near the porch."

"This isn't funny to me, Daniel. Even more reason to catch the animal if it's a skunk," Hal said urgently.

"We figure if the skunk goes in that trap you should be the one to take him out," Noah told her.

Hal studied him a long moment. "That's not fair. You're the hunters in this family."

"Coon hunters," Noah clarified.

Aunt Tootie swallowed a mouth full of food and said, "You might try throwing moth balls under the porch."

Nora looked surprised. "Your vast odd and end knowledge constantly amazes me, sister. Where did that idea come from?"

"Joe Cummings, down the road from me, did that once to get rid of skunks in his corn crib," Aunt Tootie said quickly.

"Did it work?" Jim asked.

Aunt Tootie shrugged. "I never thought to ask him."

Hal smiled at her. "Denki, Aunt Tootie. I can try the moth balls, but I still want the trap set."

Daniel said, "Just remember if you catch a skunk I will not empty it."

"You shouldn't tease your Mama Hal," scolded Nora.

Noah sided with his brother. "It should be Mama Hal's job. The skunk is in her flower bed."

Nora raised an eyebrow at John for help. He wiggled his fork at her. "Do not look at me that way. I do not like to smell like skunk."

"I won't be crazy about it, either, if that skunk stinks up my bedroom," grumbled Aunt Tootie narrowing her eyes at John.

He shrugged and concentrated on eating.

Hal met Noah's look squarely. "Fine, I give up. Just set the old trap for me."

"We will need two fresh eggs," Daniel said.

"Why?" Hal's voice had an edge to it. Her hens weren't laying so good at the moment.

"That is what a skunk likes to eat. The eggs lure him into the trap," Noah explained.

After the worship service ended, Bishop Bontrager

announced there was a member meeting. When the children and Hal's relatives left the house, Elton stated to the members it was time to give of themselves without sparing as the verse in Proverbs told them.

The members needed to plan and set the date for a barn raising frolic to be held in a week and a half. He informed Emma, as teacher, and the parents that school would be closed for a few days while the children helped.

Parents should tell their children to show up at the site of the burnt barn early a week from Monday morning. Hopefully, the barn rubble cooled off enough by then to be handled. The students could clear away the rubble, ashes and foundation blocks that weren't useful anymore.

The men loaded the bench wagon that evening. Instead of taking it to Rudy Briskey's farm for the next worship service in two weeks, the next morning Luke Yoder drove the wagon to the Stolfus farm. The benches would be unloaded to use as tables and seats for the meals during the barn raising.

The men made plans to order building supplies in the coming week. Levi Yoder was put in charge of renting a crane to come out to lift the rafters and walls.

The bishop announced Jonah Stolfus was in need of enough hay to last him through the winter since all of his burnt. Anyone with extra hay was to bring bales to the Stolfus farm as soon as the barn was built.

Rudy Briskey spoke first. "I have plenty of hay bales and will donate a wagon load."

Other farmers responded they would share their hay.

The bishop continued, "The sheriff investigated the barn fire along with the Wickenburg Fire Chief. They have reason to think the fire was arson. The sheriff said it must have been set by someone in our community since the person was riding a horse."

Rudy Briskey said in his outspoken way, "Or, the person wanted to point the finger in our direction to throw suspicion away from himself."

"This the sheriff has to find out," the bishop said. "Until he arrests the person, he said we should be watchful at all times. He expects the arsonist to strike again. No telling who might be the next target of such an unbalanced person. This is a dangerous time for Plain people."

Jonah Stolfus stood up. "I heard some harsh words about the arsonist at the salebarn and Yoder's Country Store already. I will be honest with all of you before God. As a community, our biggest weakness is we do not come together and pray for the souls of people who cause us trouble. If we could do that, maybe the light would come to the arsonist that he has done wrong. I would be the first one to go to the sheriff and say, "Just give me his hand. I will take him on home. He is one of us. Forgive without punishing it says in Colossian."

"We are supposed to practice what we preach," Bishop Bontrager said. "Jonah Stolfus is right. We should pray God intervenes and helps this man who is so tormented to come forward and atone for his wrongs. If he could see how much harm his actions have caused others, maybe he will repent."

Members nodded their heads and many said amen.

27

Chapter 3

At the noon fellowship lunch, Jim said to John, "You know I was thinking we ought to head home this week, but I've changed my mind. I just have to stay long enough to help build the barn. Nora can take pictures to show our friends when we get home."

John frowned slightly. "Make sure to tell Nora to stay back far enough that she does not get our faces in her pictures." His voice was low. Meant only for Jim.

"I'm sorry, John. I forgot that," Jim said contritely.

John waved his hand at Jim. "That is all recht. It is hard to remember sometimes the differences between our beliefs. The Plain community for generations has rebuilt burnt or destroyed barns. Plain farmers cannot do without a barn for their livestock, but we can do without praise or pictures for doing what is recht to help each other.

You were here a year ago when we repaired barns after the tornado. A barn raising is much the same except it takes longer. Building can take a week at least in good weather of dawn to dusk effort depending on the size of the barn and how much help we have.

Plain people come from miles around to help. Some have lost their own barns at one time and received help rebuilding. They remember how bad they felt about their loss. Now they are seeking to return the favor."

Bishop Bontrager swallowed his last bite and spoke. "The plan is to get the farmer's animals and hay under roof as soon as possible, both for practical and psychological reasons."

Samuel Nisely nodded in agreement. "Sure enough, a barn fire is a traumatic experience for any farm family. To see Chicken Plucker's farm animals endangered and his equipment and hay go up in smoke is a sight none of us can forget. Chicken Plucker sure enough will never forget how awful it felt."

Eli Mast added, "So far Chicken Plucker has lost two cows and a horse that were badly burnt. He is not sure how many more will die. As it is, his milk production has cut way down with so many of the cows not feeling well. That means a loss in income."

"That's really tough," Jim agreed. "Winter's coming, too. A barn on his farm would be the handiest for him, and those scorched animals need the shelter.

Knowing winter is right around the corner is why my wife, sister-in-law and me are leaving for home shortly after the barn is built. I sure don't want to drive all the long miles home in a winter storm."

"We do not blame you for we know how hard it is to travel in the winter," the bishop said. "Know we will miss your company, and hope you can come back soon. We will pray for your safe journey home."

"Thank you, Bishop. Tootie, Nora and I sure like visiting with John, Hal and our grandkids. We've made so many friends around here and will miss all of you," Jim said sincerely.

At another table, Hal passed out saucers of apple pie. She set a serving in front of Rudy Briskey while he smiled up at her. "How is your sheep doing?"

It was hard to tell if he was teasing. He knew she'd have trouble when he gave her ewes with mastitis in their bags for services rendered. She didn't know Rudy the time he insisted she go with him. She thought she was going to be a midwife for his wife. He kept talking about Martha in labor, and he sure didn't bother to correct her. Was it a coincidence that Rudy named one of his ewes after his wife? Hal suspected the ewe only carried the name Martha until after she delivered the lambs. Hal pulled the triplet lambs, and they all lived. Rudy's reason for having the nerve to ask for Nurse Hal's help was she was closer than the vet. Saving his lambs was his emergency.

Payment was two ewes. Was he really interested in how she made out with his worthless ewes? Maybe inside he was smiling at how he'd pulled the sheep's wool over her eyes.

Hal replied, "Fine, denki. They both had a set of twins. I admit I was glad to see the end of bottle feeding the lambs. That was a job, but I found I love sheep. John bought me ten more ewes and a buck at the salebarn. I'm looking forward to lambs in the spring with mothers that can take care of them this time."

"You will always have a lamb or two to feed. It might be the left out one of a set of triplets, or a confused ewe that refuses to claim her lambs. If you want to get out of bottle feeding, I have the perfect answer. Buy a milk goat," Rudy advised.

"How does buying a milk goat help me? I'd have to milk her all the time, fill the bottles and feed the lambs." Hal wondered what the catch was. John warned her with Rudy there was always a catch.

"Milk goats often will adopt bottle lambs along with their kids. Just keep the lambs in the goat's pen. Wean the lambs along with the kids and dry the goat up. Simple as that," Rudy stated.

"I see. That sounds easy. I'll discuss this with John. If he wants a goat, he can get me one at the salebarn," Hal said as she turned to go back to the kitchen.

"Wait!" Rudy exclaimed.

Hal turned around slowly.

"No need to bother with the salebarn. I own a dozen milk goats. I would gladly sell you one to help you out. Jah, I would," Rudy said smoothly.

Hal imagined Rudy would have made a good used car

salesman in another life. "I have to think about this." Hal backed up to go get more pie.

Emma was talking to Mary Mast, Eli's wife and didn't see her step mother coming until Hal bumped into her. "Oh, Emma, I'm sorry. I should watch where I'm walking." She nodded slightly toward Rudy Briskey.

Rudy waved his fork at her. "I will gladly deliver."

Emma grabbed Hal by the arm and headed for the kitchen. She whispered in Hal's ear. "What is Rudy Briskey up to now?"

"He wants to sell me a milk goat."

"Really? What did you tell him?" Emma asked, trying not to smile.

"I'd have to talk to your father," Hal said.

"Gute answer," Emma agreed. "We do need to go to the salebarn soon though. I have to help you pick out a rooster. Maybe Daed will see a gute milk goat there if you really want one."

Hal put pie filled saucers on her tray. "Jah, the sooner the better we should go to get the rooster. Tom Turkey has designated himself as ruler over the flock. I'm afraid a strange rooster will have trouble living with Tom."

"Give them plenty of room to run so the rooster can get out of Tom's way. Hopefully, they will get used to each other soon. No matter how Tom Turkey feels about it, you must have a rooster to hatch chicks," Emma declared.

"How about we go to next Wednesday's sale while you're not teaching school," Hal suggested.

"Sounds gute to me," Emma agreed. "It will be fun."

When it was the women's turn to eat, Jane Bontrager brought a woman to Hal's table. Hal saw them coming and didn't recognize the woman. She must be one of the newcomers, a dark haired, thin, stern faced woman, in her mid forties, dressed in black. The idea passed through Hal's mind that this woman should get along well with Stella Strutt for a neighbor.

"This is Wanda Bruner, Nurse Hal," Jane introduced.

"Wanda lives with her husband and her sister on the Boxholder farm. They have just arrived from Kansas."

Hal shook hands with Wanda. "Wilcom to our community. Won't you join me for lunch while we have a few seats left? Jane, you too."

"I have to finish dessert serving. Save a place for me. I will be back," Jane said over her shoulder.

"Where in Kansas did you live?" Hal asked.

Wanda placed her plate on the table and sit down. "Hutchinson, Kansas."

"I've never been to Kansas," Hal replied. "Is it much different from here?"

"Jah, much. Kansas is flat, hot and dry land. I know I will like the pretty green rolling hills around here. Iowa already feels cooler to me than Kansas," Wanda said, smiling.

Wanda's smile was sweet, and she had a soft, pleasing voice. So much for first impressions. To her surprise, Hal liked the woman. That made her sorry she'd lumped Wanda into Stella Strutt's company just because of her black clothes and the fact they were neighbors. "Sure enough. That's because it's fall. Winter will be freezing cold and seem way too long. Next summer you will appreciate the new paper fans the feed and grocery stores hand out. By then you will wonder what the difference was between Iowa and Kansas," Hal advised, returning her smile.

"Jah, that is what the real estate agent told us when we called to see if there was any farms for sale in the area," Wanda agreed. "My husband, Enoch, told the man still and all compared to Kansas, Iowa sounded much better for gute farm land and weather wise. We were told there are not as many dry spells here as in Kansas. The land is more fertile which makes for better crops."

Hal took a bite of her ham sandwich, chewed and swallowed while she thought about the Bruner family coming to live among strangers. She knew how she felt when she moved from Titonka to Wickenburg so far away from her relatives. When her parents and Aunt Tootie left for home, she'd miss them. "So that's how you decided to move here? A farm was for sale in this area."

"Sure enough, that was the final reason. Another reason is we knew the Old Order Amish in this community had a strong Ordnung. That is what we want. Too many people in our community around Hutchinson have become Beachy Amish. They bought cars and phones. They made their homes modern and live more like the English around us. With so few left in Old Order at the worship services, we felt the need to move where a larger settlement believed as we do," Wanda explained.

Hal hunched down in her seat and ate. *How would this quiet, devoutly faithful woman feel when she finds out I own a car and cell phone. That I am only allowed to use them for emergencies might not make a difference to Wanda.* "I see. You must have left many relatives behind which was hard."

Wanda's face was sad as she ran the potato salad around her plate with her fork. "Jah and friends. We were born and raised near Hutchinson. It had always been home, but we will make this our new home now."

"Gute, we will be glad to have you." Hal said.

From behind her came Bishop Bontrager's voice. "How are you ladies this fine day?"

"I'm gute, Bishop," Hal replied, twisting to look at Elton.

"I'm fine, Bishop," Wanda said.

Bishop Bontrager looked around the room. "I would like to meet your sister. Do you know where she is at recht now?"

"Gladys stayed home today. She hasn't been feeling well. I think the move was hard on her," Wanda answered.

"That is too bad. I hope she is feeling better soon. We do not want her missing too many worship services if she can help it. Do tell her I will be around to introduce myself one day this week, and see how her heath is then," the bishop said.

Wanda nodded. "Jah, Bishop. I will tell her."

"If you hadn't heard, I'm the nurse for the community. John built a medical clinic on our home, but I do make house calls. We use the clinic for birthing as well as treating patients if you or someone in your family needs help," Hal said.

Wanda said quietly, "That is gute to know."

"Would you like me to come visit your sister? Maybe I can help her feel better," Hal said.

"Nah!" Wanda said much too quickly. When Hal gave her a searching look, Wanda added calmly, "Nah, no need to bother. I think Gladys just needs to rest up."

Later that afternoon when Enoch and Wanda Bruner arrived home, Wanda said, "I should check on Gladys before I gather eggs."

She walked over to the grossdawdi house and opened the door. "Gladys?"

A tall thin woman came to meet her. "I heard you were back from church. How did it go with all those strangers?"

Wanda walked across the large room and sat in one of two rockers. She smiled cheerfully. "It went well. Enoch and I met so many nice people that I will have trouble remembering their names until I get to know them. How are you feeling now? I told everyone you were not well, but when you were better you would come to church with us."

"I feel tired all the time, but I pray I will be better soon," Gladys said, easing slowly down in the other rocker.

"Bishop Bontrager asked about you. I told him you did not feel well enough to attend the worship service, but he insisted he would be by one day this week to meet you. He wants to see for himself that you were not able to go to the service with us. I hope that your health will improve in two weeks if for no other reason than to please the bishop."

"I do not know if I will feel better by then," Gladys said.

"I met the Plain people's nurse who has a clinic in her home. Nurse Hal she is called. She offered to pay you a visit to tell you what ails you. I said I would check with you to see that would be all recht."

"William Boxholder told me about that one and her clinic when we were buying this farm. He said she was English married to a Plain man." Gladys's voice was icy.

"I wondered about that. Her speech does sounds English. Her red hair makes her stand out some, but everyone seems to like her. She has done gute work in the community so I hear from the bishop's wife," Wanda defended.

Gladys glared down her long nose at her sister. "I am not sick enough or desperate enough to use an English woman as a nurse when she pretends to be Plain."

"All recht, but she is not pretending. Nurse Hal is living a very gute life as a Plain person and raising her husband's children," Wanda said meekly.

Gladys folded her arms over her chest. "I will hear no more of her."

At her sister's tone of voice, Wanda shrank back in the rocker. "Sure enough."

Gladys patted her sister on the knee to change the mood. "Now tell me of the people at the worship service today."

Wanda straightened up and leaned forward. "They were talking about someone's burning a barn. Denki to God, no one was hurt."

"Do they know how the fire happened?" Gladys asked.

"Nah, but they know someone started it. Jonah Stolfus saw a rider on horseback leaving his farm. Bishop Bontrager asked the congregation to be watchful for such a person," Wanda said. "At the member meeting, plans were made to help build Jonah Stolfus a new barn. He will be able to milk his cows at home soon. He lost all his hay so the bishop asked for offerings to replace his loss. Rudy Briskey generously offered a whole wagon load of bales. That brought other farmers forward to offer their hay to help Jonah Briskey.

I think we made the right decision to come here, Sister. Everyone is so friendly and helpful. They all pitch together when another family needs help."

"Sounds like it. That is gute," Gladys agreed, looking at her hands in her lap.

The Lapp family arrived home from the worship service after an afternoon of visiting. Hal remembered she hadn't taken the time to check the live trap before they left for the Yoder farm. While the rest of the family went inside, she walked to the end of the porch and looked down. The trap hadn't thrown, but the two eggs had round holes broken in them and sucked dry. Beside the trap was another freshly dug hole.

Hal called, "Noah, Daniel, come out here."

The boys came out the screen door, stuffed their hands in their trouser pockets and waited.

Hal pointed toward her flower bed. "The monster under the porch has eaten two of my gute eggs and didn't throw the trap. Now it has dug another hole to by pass the trap. Do something, please!"

The boys walked to the edge of the porch and jumped off. They squatted to inspect the digging.

Noah pointed at the hole. "The animal dug that hole to get out from under the porch. I know because the dirt is on the back side the hole."

"Will the skunk come back now that he has gotten away?" Hal asked.

"Probably. The skunk seems to like his new home. Give us two more eggs, Mama Hal," Daniel said.

Noah suggested, "We could get a couple scraps of plywood and lay along this side of the porch so the animal cannot dig."

"Whatever it takes, I'm all for it," Hal said.

"We will have to lay the boards on your flowers," Noah warned.

"Do it. As you can see the flowers are ruined. It hurts me to look at them so they need to be pulled anyway," Hal said.

"We can do that for you before we lay the boards down. The plywood will lay more level," Daniel offered.

Hal stopped with her hand on the screen door handle. "While you do pull and carry the flowers off, I'll hunt up a box of mothballs to throw under the porch. We'll find out if Aunt Tootie is recht about skunks not liking the scent."

It didn't take the boys long to pull the flowers and leave with their arms full of marigold plants. Hal sat in the porch

36

swing listening to a red hen caw happily, scratching for bugs by the barn.

Biscuit lay by her feet, waiting for the boys to come back. He shot up and sniffed the air. His body tensed as he stared toward the barn.

"What do you see?" Hal looked across the driveway. "Quiet down! Nothing over there but a hen scratching in the dirt."

A growl rumbled deep in Biscuit's throat. The hair stood up on the back of his neck as he edged stiffed legged down the porch steps. Suddenly, he raced toward the hen.

Hal called, "Come back here. Don't chase my … ." She stopped when she saw the black animal with a white stripe, sneaking up on the hen. Hal looked around frantically. "Help!"

Both boys carried a scrap piece of plywood. Hal waved. "Noah and Daniel, come quick. Hurry! Biscuit is after the skunk."

Footsteps thudded on the floor inside the house. Jim looked over John's shoulder at the door. "What did you just say?"

Hal pointed a trembling finger toward the barn. "The skunk is trying to catch a hen. Biscuit is going to fight him."

"I will get the rifle," he said.

Everything after that happened so quickly. The dog ran at the skunk with a vicious snarl. The hen flew out of the way, squawking an alarm to the other chickens. The skunk jumped sideways to avoid Biscuit and scrambled toward the porch.

Biscuit was in hot pursuit. Noah and Daniel dropped their plywood and pelted the skunk with rocks which didn't help change the animal's direction.

Nora raised the living room window. "Can I help?"

"Are you crazy? Don't go out there with that skunk," Aunt Tootie ordered.

"For once, Aunt Tootie is recht. Stay in the house where you're out of that skunk's line of fire," Hal said.

"How do you like that? My niece just said I was only right once," huffed Aunt Tootie to her sister.

"That's what she said all right," Nora agreed distractedly as she watched the skunk coming closer.

Hal clapped her hands and shouted. That didn't help so she begged, "Please, skunk, don't go under the porch!" The skunk was too busy ducking rocks and out running the dog to pay attention to her. Hal resorted to prayer. "Please God don't let him go under the porch."

The cat size black blur kept coming with Biscuit right behind him. Hal feared the dog would chase the skunk up the porch steps. She climbed in the porch swing and grabbed hold of the chain to steady herself when the swing swayed.

The skunk sensed the dog right behind him. He stopped, brace his feet and lifted his tail. Biscuit skidded to a stop and took the close range spray in the face. Angry, Biscuit bit the skunk's tail, before the effects of the pew caused the dog to flatten on the ground. He whined as he rubbed his smarting eyes with his paws.

The skunk whipped around and lunged at Biscuit. He dug his claws into the dog's face and bit him. Biscuit gave a deep throated growl as he wrestled to get loose. The skunk gave up his hold.

The dog decided he was more interested in his discomfort than he was the skunk. He rubbed his face and nose with a paw where the skunk bit him. That didn't help so Biscuit tumbled across the yard, thinking he'd rub the stink off his coat.

To Hal's relief, the skunk change directions. Instead of coming up the porch steps, he ran along side the porch and came around the end. Too late, Hal screamed at him to go away, but the skunk paid her no mind as he dived down the hole.

The boys raced around the end of the porch and looked across the yard. "Where did the skunk go?" Noah asked.

"Under the porch," Hal said nasally, holding her nose.

The screen door slam behind John. He was armed with a rifle.

Hal snapped, "You're too late!"

Jim peered out the screen door. "Where's the skunk now?"

"Where else? Under the porch," Hal said tersely. Biscuit started up the steps. Hal yelled, "Stop that dog. Don't let him on the porch. He needs a gute bath before he comes up here. Check to see how bad his face wounds are. The skunk bit him."

Daniel scrunched up his face and tried not to breath deep as he grabbed the dog around the neck. "There is an open area on Biscuit's cheek where the skin is laid back, and a little blood beside his nose."

John grimaced. "That is not gute. Daniel you give the dog a bath. Noah you run to the phone shed and call the vet. Tell him what has happened and ask him what we should do."

Daniel guided the dog around the house then yelled from out back. "Noah, bring water and tomato juice."

"I'll get the water and juice for Daniel. Also, some peroxide for the wounds," Hal said. "Why does Noah need to call a vet?"

"The skunk could have rabies. It is not natural for one to come out in the day time," said John.

Hal put her hands to her face. "Ach, nah!"

When Noah came back, he panted between words as he flopped onto the couch. "The vet says if we catch the skunk he will send in his brain to be tested. It may take two weeks to get the results. We are to keep Biscuit penned up and be very careful around him until the vet gets back to us."

"I figured that. I already put Biscuit in the tool shed for recht now," John said.

Daniel stood in the kitchen door with his hands in his pockets. "I got the bath tub down from the nail in the mud room. I have already taken a bath so now you take yours before we leave for the singing. The tea kettle is hot again."

Later, Noah came back to the living room, sniffing himself. "We maybe should stay home tonight."

"You think?" Hal teased. She sniffed him. "Actually, you didn't do such a bad job of getting rid of the stink."

"I still think I smell like skunk," Noah said.

"You might, but it is not noticeable enough to miss the singing," John said.

After milking, Noah and Daniel hitched Ben to the courting buggy. He stuck his head in the screen door. "We are leaving for the singing."

Daniel was behind him. "I am riding Molly tonight."

John stopped rocking and smiled at him. "The courting buggy getting crowded."

Daniel blushed. "Jah, Noah is taking Jenny Yoder with him tonight. Mark Yoder and I will ride our horses."

Noah blushed as he quickly shut the screen door and tromped down the porch steps with Daniel hurrying to keep up.

"Your boys are growing up, John," Jim said. "Noah dating now and soon Daniel will be."

"Jah," John agreed.

Aunt Tootie came out of her bedroom with a handkerchief over her nose. "The wind is from the east. I don't know which is worse. The skunk smell on the dog, or the moth ball smell under the porch working its way into my bedroom."

Nora laughed. "Hal was desperate, but just remember the moth balls were your idea."

"Pooh," grumped Aunt Tootie as she disappeared into the clinic.

That night after they went to bed, Hal turned on her side and rested her head on her hand. "John, did you meet the new member, Enoch Bruner, at worship service?"

"Jah, I did," John uttered sleepily.

"Well, what did you think of him?" Hal insisted.

"That he was a hard working man who will make a gute living on his farm."

"I met his wife, Wanda. Her sister, Gladys Kraybill, stayed home. Not feeling well her sister said," Hal mused.

John opened his eyes and looked at her. "You do not sound as if you believe her?"

"Wanda seemed really edgy when she talked about her sister. I got the feeling there might be something else wrong. I offered to pay Gladys a visit, but Wanda shot that down quick enough," Hal said.

40

John muttered, "You suppose it might be because the woman is not ailing enough to need a nurse or doctor?"

"That's true, but she better not be faking. Bishop Bontrager told Wanda he was stopping by one day this week to meet Gladys. He wants her to the next worship service. Did Enoch tell you why they moved here after they lived in Kansas their whole life?" Hal persisted.

"Jah, the Old Order Amish was phasing out to Beachy Amish, and he wanted to go where other Old Order Amish live," John reported drowsily.

"Jah, Wanda told me that, too. I think I will have a problem with them before they have a chance to settle in." Hal let out a long sigh.

John's eyes flew open again. "Now why would you think that? You just met Wanda Bruner, ain't so?"

"Wanda said they were against owning cars and cell phones," Hal replied.

"Sure enough. That is just like our Ordnung rules," John said.

"Except I own a car and a cell phone. How is Wanda and her husband going to feel toward me when they find out?"

"If the time comes we need to, we will explain how you use the car and phone for emergencies and hope they understand. Stop worrying and go to sleep now," John grumped, throwing his arm over his eyes.

"Ach, you sound just like Jane," Hal complained.

"Sure enough, I expect I do. Jane is a smart woman," John said with a sparkle in his dark brown eyes.

"Fine, but I can't help worrying. I like Wanda. If the Bruners find out about my modern conveniences from Stella Strutt, you know how she can spin the story. It won't be in my favor."

"Nothing we can do about it this late at night. Go to sleep, Hal," came John's muffled slur as he drifted off.

Chapter 4

Monday started off routine. Everyone woke up early. The men went to the barn, and the women headed for the kitchen. Above the usual farm sounds came Biscuit's long mournful howls of protest about being locked up.

As soon as Hal dressed Redbird and Beth, she put the girls in their high chairs. "I'm going to check the live trap before I get busy and forget to do it," Hal told her mother and aunt.

She walked to the end of the porch. She could see through the trap. The broken eggs had been sucked dry, but the trap door wasn't shut. The plywood covered the flower bed. At the end of the plywood was a gaping hole. Hal groaned.

At breakfast, she gave the boys an update. "I will give the animal credit for being industrious. It tunneled under the plywood to get out. Now what do we do? There has to be a way to outsmart the critter."

Noah stopped eating to think. "We have a rock pile in the gully where we picked up rocks out of the fields. Suppose we lined the rocks along the plywood. The animal would find those too heavy to move, and the rocks should sink on top of him if he digs under them."

"If that's what it's going to take, I'll gladly help you carry the rocks," Hal said. "That animal has to find a new home before winter. I don't want it to hibernate under the porch."

42

"Not that I will be here this winter, but I agree with Hallie," Aunt Tootie said. "I am uncomfortable with the notion that an animal is living that close to me. Especially a skunk."

Tuesday before daylight, Hal woke to the most unpleasant odor. She got out of bed and went to investigate. John followed her. The others were in the hall, holding their noses.

When everyone came downstairs, Aunt Tootie was upright in bed with a hanky over her nose. She hacked and swallowed hard which choked her.

Hal asked, "Are you all right?"

"I can't take much more of this. It smells like skunk," Aunt Tootie gasped.

"I know it does. Now which do you think smells worse, skunk stink or moth balls?" Nora teased.

Aunt Tootie's alarm clock went off. Perturbed at Nora, she slapped at the clock. Her finger slipped off the alarm clock button and bumped her cell phone. It clattered to the floor.

"Do something someone?" Aunt Tootie demanded, holding her stomach and gagging.

Nora grabbed her under the arm. "Calm down, Tootie. Next, you'll throw up. Get up and come out to the living room with me before that happens."

"I will go check the trap," Daniel said. He turned on a flashlight and eased out the clinic door. Instantly, he rushed back inside. "We caught the skunk. What do we do, Noah?"

"We did not catch the skunk. Mama Hal did," Noah said with a wink.

"You aren't serious about making me empty that trap," Hal moaned.

"Jah, that is recht. That was the deal. We catch the skunk, and you empty the trap," Daniel said.

"All recht, but I have to find me some clothes to wear that I can air out and wash," Hal grumped, shaking the skirt of her cotton nightgown.

"Come on, Noah. We better get to the barn and start the generator." Daniel headed for the door.

"Will you people please hurry up and decide what you're

going to do," Aunt Tootie whined, standing in the door way. "This is terrible. I'm getting so sick at my stomach."

A series of rings in the cupboard interrupted her tirade. Everyone stared at the cupboard door.

"That has to be my cell phone. I wasn't expecting a call from anyone," Hal exclaimed. She fished the phone out of her nursing bag and flipped the lid. "Hello." An outburst of giggling met her ear. "Good morning, Nurse Hal. This is Jean in the emergency center at the sheriff's office. Sounds like you have an emergency at your house." Jean burst into laughter again. "I'm sorry. I know it isn't funny to you."

"And you are calling me, why?" Hal asked dryly. She usually had a sense of humor but not this morning.

"Someone at your house called nine one one. I couldn't get anyone to talk to me, but I can hear the excitement going on and recognized your voice. I decided to call your phone, so you knew we were listening in."

"I am so sorry we bothered you," Hal apologized, blushing.

Jean choked on laughter. "No problem. I'm just glad it's you and not me that has to empty that trap."

"Thanks a lot," Hal said.

"You really shouldn't call nine one one for evacuating a skunk from a trap," Jean cautioned seriously.

"Of course not. I'll be sure to deliver your message to the one that made the call. I'm so sorry we bothered you." After she hung up, Hal looked from her mother to her aunt. "Which one of you called nine one one about the skunk? You got us in trouble with the emergency center."

The women looked innocently at each other and shrugged.

Hal fisted her hands on her hips. "I'm to tell the caller a skunk in a trap wasn't the kind of emergency the center handles. Both of you check your phones, please."

"Hal, my phone is upstairs. I haven't touched it for a long time," Nora declared.

Tootie snatched up her phone from the floor and checked it. "Uh oh!" Tootie eased the phone to her ear. Quickly, she shut it off. "Someone was laughing on the other end."

"Aunt Tootie!" Hal screeched.

"I'm sorry, Hal. I didn't know when the phone fell it speed dialed itself nine one one," Aunt Tootie said sheepishly.

Hal turned to face John. "John, about the skunk."

"Oh no, I cannot take care of the skunk. I have to milk, and the cows will not come in the milk room if I smell like skunk," John said.

"Dad?"

"It's daylight now. I have to help John milk," Jim said, lining up with John and the boys.

"All of you are cowards. Fine, I will empty the trap. First, I have to change into some old clothes."

"You can use a pair of my old trousers and a shirt," John offered.

"That's generous of you," Nora said dryly.

John shrugged as he grinned at her. He headed for the barn with Jim following him.

Hal rushed from the room. She came back in a few minutes in one of John's blue work shirts and black trousers. She'd put on her oldest black bonnet over her prayer cap to cover her hair. A black work hanky covered her nose and mouth. A pair of yellow chore gloves protected her hands. She held up John's twenty-two rifle. "Wish me luck, ladies."

"You should find something to throw over the trap to keep the skunk from pewing you. The stink will get on you bad enough from just handling the trap and being near that animal," Nora said.

"Sure enough. I'll get an old sheet out of the rag basket." Hal rushed off and came back carrying a folded sheet. She leaned the rifle against the wall and unfolded the sheet just enough to cover the trap. "Now I'm ready. Pray for me."

Aunt Tootie cried, "We will, dear."

Hal took a deep breath and walked outside.

Nora and Aunt Tootie rushed to the clinic window to watch. Hal threw the sheet over the side of the porch. She eased over to look down at the trap. With a grim expression,

45

she looked at her mother and aunt. "I've got the trap covered."

Hal walked down the steps and along the porch, She felt for the middle of the live trap and eased the handle upright to lifted it. The trap felt light. The skunk sure didn't weigh much.

Now where should she take the trap? Maybe to the edge of the hay field. She'd shoot the skunk and dump the body in the gully.

Hal tried not to take more than small gasps as she hurried along the lane. From the pasture drifted the bleats of her sheep flock, wanting her attention. This was no time to stop and inspected the ewes and buck like she usually would.

Somewhere she'd heard or read a skunk has to brace his feet to pew. She surely didn't have to worry about that with him off balance until she set the trap down.

When Hal reached the edge of the alfalfa, she looked around. The day was going to be a nice one. Why did this old skunk have to ruin it?

Hal eased the trap to the ground. She grabbed a hand full of sheet and pointed the rifle, ready to whip the sheet off the trap. She hesitated when she thought about what came next. This wasn't going to be easy, killing an animal. She'd never killed a living thing before except for chickens, and she cringed each time she swung the hatchet toward a chicken neck. She couldn't possible fire the rifle with the skunk looking at her. Maybe she could shoot the skunk through the sheet. She wouldn't have to see him die. She'd wait a few minutes and carry the trap to the gully to empty it.

That was the best plan Hal could come up with. She tried to steady the rifle in her trembling hands as she stuck the barrel close to the sheet. With her eyes closed, Hal squeezed the trigger. The bullet rented a round hole, with a powder burn ring, in the sheet. What if she didn't kill the skunk? The poor animal had to be in pain. She should fire once more. She closed her eyes and pulled the trigger again.

Noah was washing a cow's bag when he heard the shot. He stood up and looked at Daniel behind him. "That was a gun shot close by."

"I heard it," Daniel said as he strained to listen above the hum of the generator.

Another shot!

John and Jim stopped unhooking milkers. John said, "Maybe we better go see what the shooting is all about."

"Daniel and me can go see if you want, Daed. That way you can finish milking," Noah suggested.

John grimaced. "I do not want you walking up on hunters chasing deers. You might get shot by accident."

"John, you go with the boys. I'll milk while you're gone," Jim said.

"That might be best," John agreed. He rushed outside with the boys behind him.

Nora and Aunt Tootie stood on the edge of the porch with hands shading their eyes as they stared toward the pasture lane.

"You women hear shots?" John asked.

"Yes." Nora pointed. "Hal killed the skunk by the hay field.

"Oh, that's what it was. We might as well go back and finish milking," John said to the boys.

Noah grabbed Daniel's arm as they followed their father. "Ach, nah!"

Daniel looked confounded. "How could Mama Hal shoot the skunk? I killed the skunk."

John stopped and turned to face them. "I thought you said Hal had to empty the trap."

"We were just teasing her," Noah said. "We did not mean for her to really get rid of the skunk."

"Jah, I bopped the skunk before we went to the barn," Daniel said. "The trap is empty."

"You boys are going to be in trouble sure enough. You should have told Hal before she carried that trap off," John scolded.

"We thought she would see the trap was empty," Noah said.

Daniel puzzled, "How could she not see the trap was

empty?"

Noah and John shrugged.

John said, "I think we better go check on her."

Hal laid the rifle on the ground. She'd have to take the sheet off to open the trap. What if that skunk wasn't dead? Maybe she missed it. The skunk would pew her.

She'd just throw the trap, skunk and all in the gully. The boys could go get it later. She picked the trap up.

"Hal, you all recht?" John asked. He tried not to smile when he saw the bullet holes in the sheet.

Noah put his hand over his mouth. His eyes twinkled when he winked at Daniel.

Daniel frowned. He feared in a minute they wouldn't think this was so funny when Mama Hal was mad at them.

Hal whirled around. Tears streamed down her face as she set the trap on the ground. "John, now what do I do? I shot the skunk twice, but I have to figure out how to get him out of the trap. I don't know if I killed him. The poor thing might be in pain, suffering because I shot him."

John put his arms around Hal so she could see his face. He winked at the boys. "I do not see how you could have missed at such close range."

"We can empty the trap for you, Mama Hal," Noah said eagerly.

Daniel stared hard at his brother. "Noah?"

Noah elbowed him and gave a slight shake of his head. "Come on, Daniel. Mama Hal was brave to do this much. We will get rid of the skunk for her."

"Sure enough," Daniel declared, catching on to Noah's notion. He picked up the trap with the sheet still covering it.

Stepping away from John, Hal confessed, "I was going to dump him in the gully."

"A gute place to take the skunk," Noah said. "Go with me, Daniel."

John took the rifle from her. "Come on, Hal. You need to take a bath before breakfast. You do not smell pretty gute." He

48

put his arm around her waist and walked down the pasture lane.

When they passed the tool shed, Biscuit's frantic barking made Hal remember. "John, we have to go back to get the skunk. The vet will need the brain to test for rabies so we can let that poor dog be free again."

"I did forget. You go on in and take your bath. I will tell the boys to bring the skunk back here for the vet," John told her as he turned to go back down the lane.

He met the boys. "Where did you really throw the skunk? The vet has to come get the brain for testing."

"We know," Noah said. "We threw the skunk behind the tool shed. I was going to call the vet as soon as we finished chores."

"How's Mama Hal?" Daniel asked.

"Very unhappy with herself, but she remembered we needed the skunk brought back to the house. She sent me to tell you to fetch it," John said.

At breakfast, Nora and Aunt Tootie praised her for her bravery to get rid of the beast that trampled her flowers and dug holes in her flower bed. Both women darted scalding looks at Noah and Daniel for being so mean and watched them squirm for making Hal get rid of the skunk.

That morning while the boys helped fix fence, Noah said to his father, "I think we better tell Mama Hal we got rid of the skunk. She might feel better if she knows she did not shoot the animal."

"We did not know she was going to take it so hard when she thought she killed the skunk," Daniel said.

"You better give this more thought, boys. In a few days, the scent will be gone. The women will have other things on their minds, and Hal will forget about the skunk," Jim cautioned.

"But, Dawdi, …," Noah started.

John put a warning hand up. "Jim is recht. Hal will not like knowing you boys played a mean joke on her. She is better off thinking she killed the skunk even though it hurts her."

49

"I feel so guilty," Daniel said.

"Live with it," John declared.

"We should not lie. God will not like it," Daniel persisted.

John thought a moment. "Daniel, what you did was not a lie. You teased Mama Hal, and she misunderstood. There is a difference."

Jim stopped hammering on a staple. "Keep what you did in mind the next time you want to play a trick on anyone."

"We did not plan on playing a trick on Mama Hal," Noah declared.

"Maybe she will understand if we explain," Daniel said hopefully. "If she had only looked over the porch at the trap before she threw the sheet on it. She could have seen the trap was empty."

"I would not count on Hal seeing this your way. Not yet," John warned.

Jim added, "Maybe not ever."

Chapter 5

Tuesday night was cloudy with a chance of rain. The raw air had a chilled dampness to it, but that didn't matter. This was the perfect night for a midnight ride if the rider didn't want to be seen. Mounting the work horse was hard with a sore leg. Staying on the hard stepping horse was even more difficult when the throbbing pain increased, but Rudy Briskey's farm wasn't far away. What did the pain matter? It was nothing to suffer pain compared to getting the task at hand completed.

Rudy Briskey needs to be taught a lesson for giving Jonah Stolfus all that hay. How was my burning Jonah Stolfus's barn teaching the man a lesson if Rudy Briskey gives him hay for the winter? His charity encouraged other farmers to do the same.

Rudy Briskey had a large cornfield on the south side his property. With the draft horse at a quiet walk, the rider moved past the Briskey home. The windows were dark as they should be that time of night.

Just south of the house, was the cornfield. The driveway was at the northern end of the field which was good. Corn shocks loomed out of the darkness in no particular pattern but easy to get at. The gunny sack slung across the horse's back held small juice bottles filled with kerosene and a box of matches. All the supplies needed to teach Rudy Briskey a lesson he wouldn't soon forget. The rider stopped the horse by

51

the first corn shock just inside the gate hole.

I will sprinkle kerosene on the shock. It will not take much to ignite. The corn leaves are dry. I have to be careful how much kerosene I use. I do not want to run out before I finish what I started.

At arm's length the kerosene drizzled down the dry stalks, filling the air with the scent of the fuel.

I need to move the horse ahead before I throw the match in the fire so Jack will not get scared and run off.

Scratching a match on the side the box made a raspy noise that seemed loud in the silence. A quick toss, and the flaming match lit in the shock. As the flame took hold and grew taller, the fire became brighter. The rider felt the heat and was satisfied the deed worked out well.

Now to do the same to the next shock and the next.

Soon a dozen shocks lit up with shooting flames against the dark sky, and dense gray smoke crept like fog across the field. The smoky surroundings with flaring flames turning the smoke red reminded the rider of the sun trying to burn off a thick ground fog.

The fires make it too easy to be seen. Got to get out of here and go home by way of Bender Creek Timber. My leg hurts too much to stay on this horse much longer. Got to get home. Got to get in bed.

The dark silhouette of the small wooden building known as the phone shed came into view at the intersection. The rider slowed the horse, debating whether to set the shed on fire.

Nah, this time it will not matter. The field is burning so fast the damage will be done before the firetrucks can get here. I must not waste my time. I need to get home.

When the sheep, goats, horses and cattle complained loud enough in unison, Rudy woke up, wondering what was wrong. His sheep and goats gave terrified bleats that mingled with the horses terrified screams and the cattle bellows.

The dogs ran back and forth in the yard, barking ferociously. His first thought was coyotes or wild dogs were in

52

his flock. He scrambled from the bed. As he picked up his rifle, Martha, asked, "What is going on out there?"

From the doorway, Rudy said, "I do not know, but I am about to find out."

When he stepped out into the cool darkness, Rudy smelled smoke. That's when he saw the bottom half of the cornfield a blaze. The fire spread fast across the field eating up the dry grassy rows full of corn stubbles. While Rudy watched another row of shocks went up in a blaze. A brisk south breeze fanned the flames driving the fire closer to his house.

Rudy hurried inside to put on his trousers and shoes so he could run to the phone shed down the road to call the fire department. "Martha, get dressed and keep an eye on the corn field. It is on fire."

"Ach, nah," Martha cried as she hurriedly dressed.

"I'm going to the phone shed to call the fire department. Our house and barn are in the path of the fire. Hitch up the buggy and be prepared to leave fast."

As Rudy ran to the phone shed, Martha ran to the barn. She bridled a horse and backed him up to the buggy. Once she had the harness in place, she drove away from the house. She stopped in the road to watch. She prayed for the fire to be put out before it reached her home.

In a few minutes, Rudy emerged out of the smoke that surrounded the buggy, panting from his run to the phone and back. He climbed in beside Martha, squeezed her trembling hand and leaned back against the seat to wait.

Soon the fire trucks raced to Amish country for the second time in a few days. Sirens blared and strobe lights whirled as they came to the aid of Rudy Briskey.

Wednesday morning, Emma drove to the Lapp farm. When she turned into the driveway, Emma was glad to see Noah and Daniel had taken the time to put up their farmer's market stand. They already had some of the early items laid out. The gourds for bird houses and acorn squash along with the last of the summer squash. It wouldn't be long before the pumpkins would be orange enough to pick. A quart canning jar was on the counter to put money in, on the honor system, when they weren't home.

As soon as Emma arrived, John said it was time to go. Once everyone was in the enclosed buggy, he set off at a brisk pace to the salebarn for the day.

The buggy was almost to the black top intersection when they heard a loud thud under the buggy.

"What was that I wonder?" John asked.

Hal stuck her head out the open side window. "I don't see anything."

Daniel called from the back, "I do. We ran over a black cat. He's smashed in the road behind us."

"Oh dear, that is unlucky," Aunt Tootie declared, holding her hands to her cheeks.

"Why is that, Aendi?" Noah asked.

"It is always unlucky to have a black cat cross your path," Aunt Tootie told him.

Nora shook her head disapprovingly. "Tootie, you shouldn't tell the children old superstitions."

"That is all recht, Nora. I believe Aendi Tootie is recht. It is unlucky," John said, grinning over his shoulder at her.

"You do, John?" It surprised Hal that he would say such a thing.

"It sure is unlucky," John agreed. "For the cat."

Jim slapped his leg and laughed. "You got that right."

Everyone but Aunt Tootie laughed.

"That's not how the superstition is supposed to work," Aunt Tootie said, pouting.

"How does it work?" Noah asked.

Tootie opened her mouth to respond.

Nora grabbed her sister's arm and interrupted. "Never mind, Tootie. The children don't need to learn your old wives tales."

John drove the buggy across the salebarn parking lot to the far edge and parked next to the last buggy in line at the hitching posts. Sale day was one of those special days when the work at home was left behind. The whole family enjoyed some aspect of the sale. Maybe it was visiting with friends or checking out the current prices of livestock. The salebarn was a good place to buy replacement animals. For the women and children, the small livestock sale was a must. Hal heard the sale referred to by one English woman as Old McDonald's farm sale.

The Lapp family's interest was certainly varied that day. John and Jim wanted to watch the sheep and goat sale and the cattle sale. The boys left to hang out with their friends. The women wanted to go with Hal to look for a rooster.

Before everyone scattered, Hal suggested the family meet at the Amish diner behind the ring at noon for lunch. John and Jim sit next to Amos Coblentz near the top of the wooden seats built to the bottom around the ring. The blue eyed widower was still on the school board with John. He nodded a greeting at John and Jim.

John nodded back. "Nice day for a sale, ain't so?"

"Jah," Amos said.

"What do you know?" John asked.

Amos's face turned solemn. "Did you hear Rudy Briskey's cornfield caught on fire last night?"

"Nah, I hate to hear that," John replied.

"That's kind of strange," Jim said. "We didn't have any lightning last night."

John agreed. "You are recht, Jim. Makes me wonder how such a fire happened."

"Jah, me, too. I saw the field as I drove by to come here so I got curious and stopped in to ask about the fire," Amos said. "Rudy lost most of his winter feed, before the fire trucks arrived. Gute thing he has a gute supply of hay in the barn.

Rudy told me the firemen were sure the fire was deliberately set. With the wind from the south last night, the fire burned close to the house before the firemen put it out."

"Good thing the firemen got there as quick as they did," Jim said.

"Jah, gute that the animals made so much noise they woke Rudy Briskey up. His house could have burnt with him and Martha in it if he had slept too long," Amos related.

"Praise the Lord for Rudy and Martha's safety," John said.

Jim and Amos agreed at the same time. "Amen."

"As it was, smoke damage was bad inside the house," Amos told them. "It will make work for his wife airing out everything and washing curtains and clothes."

Conversations ended as the auctioneer tested his microphone so the sheep and goat sale could begin.

The small animal sale room was behind a door back of the main sale room. The room was bustling with as many people as the other room, but not farmers interested in livestock replacement or selling stock. Amish and English people crowded the room, looking for a bargain. Mostly women and children with more elderly men.

Prospective buyers walked around the two lines of tables, checking out what was for sale. On one table were stacks of egg cartons full of red eggs. Next baked goods such as loaves of bread, dinner rolls, bumble berry pies, angel food cakes and oatmeal applesauce cookies. Right next to the bake goods were small boxes of late hatched chickens and ducks.

The other table held starter plants and flower bulbs plus odd and ends usually found at yard sales.

Around the sides of the sale arena, a row of collapsible wire pens held puppies, kittens, fresh born calves from dairy farms and fall born lambs and kid goats.

At the end of the pens, plastic milk crates with wire covers and dog carriers contained rabbits, chickens, ducks, geese and turkeys.

The calliope of noises filled the room from all the unhappy, imprisoned animals and fowl which mixed with human chatter and laughter. Emma heard roosters crow and directed Hal to the chicken cages first thing. Four roosters, each in a plastic milk crate, were at the end of the line.

Hal put her hands to her cheeks. "Oh my, so many choices. I don't know which rooster to bid on."

Emma leaned down to inspect each one. "We know the rooster should be young to have gute hatches. He should be fairly large. You will have nice sized fryers that way."

"The bigger the better size wise for the rooster that has to bluff out Tom Turkey I'm thinking," Hal suggested.

"That too," Emma agreed.

"I don't want a mean one that will attack me. I've seen the way Margaret Yoder's rooster comes at her when she gathers eggs. It's not funny," Hal declared.

"Agreed, but that is a hard trait to find out about when the roosters are penned in a small cage," Emma told her. "Do you see one you like?"

Hal looked at each of the roosters. She pointed to the one on the end. The black and red feathers on that rooster shimmered as he stood as tall as he could in cramped quarters. His long, flourishing tail swiped the crate side. "Him."

"Why?" Emma asked.

"He is the prettiest," Hal said.

"After all I said, you are looking for the prettiest rooster?" Emma asked in disdain.

Hal folded her arms over her chest. "Fine, I told you I'm not much good at this. You're the chicken expert in this family so you pick one for me. I'll be happy with which ever rooster you think is suitable."

Emma broke into a smile. "Actually, he is the one I like, too. My reasons were just a bit more practical than yours is all. Now we get a seat and wait. It is up to you to bid on him."

Hal looked flustered. "You bid for me please."

"Ach, nah, this is your rooster. About time you get used to bidding at an auction. Is Daed going to buy you that milk goat today?"

Hal shook her head. "Nah, I haven't gotten up the nerve to talk to him about it yet. I wasn't sure what he'd think of the idea. It took your father some getting used to when I brought home the sheep."

Emma giggled. "I remember."

Hal's patience wore thin as she watched the sale drag on. It took forever for the auctioneer to get through the items on the table and start along the row of cages. Of course, he started on the opposite end from the poultry with the small animals and worked toward the chickens.

When the auctioneer's helper held up the rooster Hal liked, she bid and rebid every time the auctioneer looked her way. Finally, he looked at her for one last time. "Sold to the woman in the third row. What is your number?"

Hal held up the card she got from the office with the number fifty six on it.

When the auctioneer moved on, Emma said, "Gute job, Hallie. You now have a new rooster."

"And a nice looking one at that," Nora said, readjusting wiggling Redbird on her lap.

"I think he's very pretty, dear," Aunt Tootie agreed.

"What a relief to get that over with. I didn't understand a word that auctioneer said. He talked too fast," Hal declared, struggling to get Beth to sit still.

The others laughed at her.

"John's sure to ask me what the rooster cost. Did I bid too much?" Hal worried.

"Not if you really want that rooster, dear," Aunt Tootie said diplomatically.

Hal frowned at her aunt and looked questioningly at her mother.

Nora said innocently, "Don't ask me, Hallie. I don't know what's too much to give for a chicken."

Hal turned to Emma for her response.

Emma answered honestly, "To be on the safe side, pray that Daed does not ask."

Hal didn't like the sound of that answer. She groaned.

Noah and Daniel didn't have any trouble finding boys their age hanging around outside. The rumspringa crowd lingered near the lean-to sales booths along the outside the salebarn.

Albert Jostle stuck his hands in his pockets and sauntered toward Noah and Daniel, giving off a take me or leave me attitude. "Look who showed up will you, boys?"

Following behind Albert, his brothers, Will and Sam was Mark Bender, Rueban Rogies and Matthew Stoll. They all greeted the boys.

"Did you decided to come to the party Friday night on Bender Creek Road? Anyone is welcome. We could fix you both up with a girl if you want. You know the kind that don't mind taking a walk in the underbrush." Albert gave an exaggerated wink.

"We are not sure yet what we will do Friday night," Noah said, blushing as he kicked a rock with the toe of his shoe. "Recht now Daniel and I are going to look in the concession stands to see what is for sale."

"Same old junk," Matthew Stoll said as the boys walked along the stands with the Lapp brothers.

One booth counter was piled with stacks of quilts of various sizes and designs, all in black, blue and purple colors. Another held bake goods like doughnuts, cookies and bread. The next one had small jars of jams, jellies, molasses and honey.

Daniel said, "We can get any of these things at home for free."

Noah nodded and stopped at a stand that had battery operated calculators and radios on the counter beside different sizes and colors of flashlights. Next was a handy display of batteries to fit all the sale items.

Rueban Rogies pointed to a small transistor radio with a little carry strap. "I bought one of these and the batteries about a month ago. It has AM and FM channels and comes with an earplug so no one but me can hear the radio play."

"Deacon Rogies lets you keep it?" Daniel asked in surprise.

"He does not know I have it. The radio fit in my pocket until I got home. I keep it on a rafter in the hay loft."

"What do you listen to?" Noah asked.

Rueban said, "Country western music and baseball games mostly."

Noah picked the radio up and looked it over. He was very tempted. He hesitated. His father wouldn't like him to own the radio. Still if Deacon Rogies hadn't found Rueban's yet, chances were he might be able to hide a radio on a rafter and get away with it. Noah reached into his trouser pocket for his money.

Daniel grabbed his arm. "You should think about this. Buying that radio will get you in trouble with Daed sure enough."

"Not if we are the only two that know I have it," Noah said.

Daniel shrugged. "It is your money and maybe your hide."

Back home, Hal climbed out of the buggy. She reached up to take the rooster cage from Emma and place it on the ground. While Hal turned to help Aunt Tootie down, the rooster stretched his neck and crowed a hello greeting to the farm.

Tom Turkey's long neck stretched in the air to look around. When he heard the crow of a stranger, he scattered the hens he was with as he raced to the crate. Tom lowered his head and peered through the square holes as he bristled his feathers. After he had a good look at the rooster, he straightened and backed up. He stared at the cage while he stomped a foot in warning. The turkey fanned his tail and gobbled a complaint as he circled the cage, causing the rooster to growl and peck the crate.

Aunt Tootie backed up behind the buggy, ready to run for the house. She shook her finger at the turkey. "Oh dear, Tom looks mad."

Emma waved her apron tail at Tom, backing him up a few feet. "Shoo! That's not a very nice wilcom for the new rooster!"

Noah frowned. "Mama Hal, Tom is not going to let you turn the rooster loose. He is asking for a fight already. The way the rooster is bristling up, I think he is willing to oblige."

"I do not think the rooster can win in a fight with Tom," Daniel surmised.

"Fudge! What are we going to do?" Hal asked.

"Put Tom in the barn for a few days until the rooster gets

used to the farm. That way he will have time to find places to get out of Tom's reach," Daniel suggested.

"Just make sure that turkey stays in the pen room. I do not want him pestering the milk cows when we milk," John warned.

"Sure enough," Noah said. "Help me get Tom in the barn, Daniel."

Noah and Daniel herded the turkey to the barn. Daniel opened the door. Curious now, Tom forgot about the rooster as he craned his neck to look inside. This was a new place for him to check out. He hopped in and wandered around.

"What are you going to name your rooster, Hallie?" Emma asked.

Hal paused to think. "I hadn't thought about a name. How about Joseph?"

"Why Joseph?"

"Because the rooster has a coat of many colors," Hal replied.

"Sure enough," Emma agreed.

Noah hitched up Emma's buggy for her, and she left for home. The women went to the house to fix supper. While John and Jim was busy in the milk room, Noah climbed to the loft and stood on a stack of bales to reach the top side of a rafter. He fished the radio out of his trouser pocket and placed it next to a beam so he could easily find it. When he came back to the milk room to help, Daniel raised an eyebrow at him. Noah winked.

In the kitchen, Aunt Tootie said, "While you ladies get prepared for supper, I'd be glad to go gather the eggs."

"That is great," Hal said. "Thank you, Aunt Tootie."

After the mudroom door closed, Hal gave her mother a wide eyed expression. "Aunt Tootie has never offered to gather eggs. Why now?"

Nora giggled. "You should be wise to your aunt by now. My dear sister likes to pick and choose the tasks she volunteers to do. At this moment, she thinks gathering eggs is the easier one."

Aunt Tootie swung the egg bucket back and forth to scare the chickens out of her way. The hens cackled and scurried to keep from getting hit. Tootie narrowed her eyes to see into the dark hen house. Just two hens on the nests which beat half a dozen or better. She should scare the hens off the nest, but she wasn't going to bother two. She excused they might still be trying to lay. If they had an egg under them, Hal would never miss one or two eggs from this gathering. Tomorrow Hal could bring the extra eggs. The hens would peck if Aunt Tootie stuck her hand under them, and she didn't like to get peck.

She walked along the three tiers of empty nesting boxes and gently put the eggs into the bucket. That job didn't take long. She could walk slowly on the way back to the house to kill a little more time while Hallie and Nora cooked. She was wore out from the day's outing to town.

The strong sun beamed in the west, making it hard to see. Aunt Tootie squinted, trying to be careful where she put her feet. She didn't want to trip over a stick or lose her balance on unleveled ground. Plus, she'd sure hate to step in something nasty smelling that she'd have to wash off her shoe soles.

Somewhere close behind her came an awful growling noise. Aunt Tootie turned around. The new rooster, with his head stretched out, was racing at her. Joesph meant business. Tom wasn't the only one he didn't want around.

Aunt Tootie trotted toward the house, making little eeking noises. She had to stop to open the screen door. When she did, the rooster caught up to her. He flogged the calf of her legs with his spurs and pecked her. Aunt Tootie let out a scream as she squeezed through the open door.

Hal and Nora were to the mud room in a second.

"What's wrong, Aunt Tootie?" Hal asked.

Aunt Tootie leaned against the screen door, panting and waving her hand in front of her flushed face. The rooster struck the back side of the screen, flogging the door. Aunt Tootie jumped away and placed the egg bucket on the floor. She glared at Hal. "Your old rooster chased me and pecked my legs."

"Surely not," Nora said. "He must have thought you had some corn in the bucket to feed him."

"I tell you that mean thing wasn't interested in what was in the bucket." Aunt Tootie twisted at the waist, hiked up her skirt and looked at her legs. "See, I'm bleeding. Last time I gather the old eggs at this place."

"I am so sorry," Hal took Aunt Tootie by the arm when the elderly woman stuck out her lower lip in a pout. "Come sit in the kitchen and rest. I'll wash your legs and put bandages on the wounds."

That evening after everyone called it a night, Hal said softly to her husband's back, "John, are you asleep yet?"

He grumbled, "Almost. Was ist letz?"

"John, I need to buy a milk goat," Hal responded fast.

John whipped over on his side. "What did you just say?"

"I need to buy a milk goat," Hal repeated slower this time.

John sat up in bed with his eyes opened wide. "Where did that idea come from?"

"Rudy Briskey mentioned it to me at the fellowship lunch," Hal said quietly.

John rubbed his forehead like he felt a headache coming on. "I might have known. Why does Rudy think you need a milk goat?"

"Rudy said I wouldn't have to bottle feed lambs in the spring if I had a goat. If I penned her up with her babies in the barn, she'd claim orphan lambs," Hal explained, looking hopeful.

"Let me guess. Rudy has the perfect milk goat. He is willing to sell it to you to help you out," John said wearily.

"Jah, that's what he said," Hal agreed.

John eyed her in the dark. "What did you tell him?"

"That I'd have to ask you about it. If it helps any, he says he will deliver," Hal added as an incentive to help John decide in her favor.

"You have your sheep bred already. The milk goat will not do you any good if it is not bred yet. She has to kid when the lambs are due," John explained.

"Rudy said the goat is bred already," Hal assured him.

"I never know about Rudy and his deals. It seems there is always a catch, but if you want to try a milk goat who am I to say nah," John said.

Hal said excitedly, "Oh, denki, John."

"Just one goat. No more even if Rudy thinks you need a herd," John ordered.

"Recht, I understand," Hal agreed.

"The goat has to have a sound milk bag, or you will be feeding her kids on the bottle next spring along with lambs. If you go through with this, I want to go with you to inspect the goat, before you buy it. No sight unseen deals. Especially with Rudy Briskey," John instructed. He yawned as he flopped back down. Groggily, he said, "Could the rest of this talk wait until morning?"

Hal smiled and kissed John's cheek. "Jah, we can talk more about goats tomorrow. Go to sleep."

Chapter 6

The following day at breakfast, John and Jim talked about the fire that wiped out most of Rudy Briskey's corn shocks. John said Jim and he should drive over and check out the damage. He'd like to hear from Rudy if the sheriff investigated yet and had an idea how the fire started.

Hal laid her fork on her plate as she added, "I really should go along to help Martha with the house cleaning."

"Gute idea. Amos said it will be a chore for her to get rid of the smoke smell in the whole house," John said.

"I can go along and help if that's all right. Three of us will get done faster than two," Nora said. "How about you, Tootie? Want to go with us to clean the house."

"I don't do well in smoky places with my bad breathing." Aunt Tootie put her hand over her mouth to cover a weak cough. "Besides, my legs are sore from the rooster bites. How about I stay here with the girls?"

"Sounds gute to me," Hal agreed. "They don't need to be in that smoke, either."

Later when John drove by Rudy Briskey's burnt cornfield, he shook his head. "What a waste is that."

"It is," Jim agreed.

"How could anyone think it was a fun game to start fires like this," Hal declared.

"Someone who is sick," Jim said simply as John parked by the house.

Rudy came out of the barn to greet them. "Wilcom. Get down. It is nice to see you. What brings you here this fine day?"

Hal climbed down and picked up her cleaning basket from the back. "Gute Morgen, Rudy. Mom and I are going to help Martha. Come on, Mom. Let's get Martha's house back in order." She rushed her mother away from the men, knowing that Rudy would delay them if he thought about selling her that goat.

Martha came out on the porch with a broom in her hand. "Wilcom, but you might not want to come into my smoky house."

"That's exactly where we're headed," Hal said, smiling. "Mom and I want to help you clean."

Martha held the door for them. "That is very kind of you. I would appreciate the help."

The ladies divided up the cleaning detail. Hal washed the windows on the outside while Nora washed the inside glasses. Martha had scrubbed the floors before they got there, and now she started washing the gray smudge off the walls.

While Hal and Nora washed all the pots, pans and dishes, Martha cooked their lunch. By the time John, Jim and Rudy came in, the women were ready to sit down and almost too tired to eat.

That afternoon while the women finished washing the walls, Martha said to Hal, "You plan on cooking molasses this fall?"

"Jah, the boys mowed the grass at Sugar Camp this morning. This afternoon they're cutting a stack of wood to burn under the vat. After that, we will be ready to start," Hal said.

"You let me know when you are ready. I will help cook the molasses for your help here," Martha told her.

"That is nice of you to offer, but stirring over the vat is such a hot job. If you help, you can share the molasses," Hal told her.

66

The afternoon flew by. By the time, the Lapp family was ready to go home Martha's house was smelling much better.

Rudy and Martha walked to the buggy with them. Rudy cleared his throat to get their attention. "Nurse Hal, have you decided about getting a milk goat yet. I have one penned up in the barn for you to look at."

Hal glanced at John. "I left it up to John to decide."

"So you really want to get a goat, Hal?" John just remembered the sleepy conversation he'd had with Hal.

"Only if you think she will be useful in the spring when I need milk for the lambs," Hal said not wanting to seem pushy.

"I penned one up in the barn. You are wilcom to look at her. I will give you a gute deal on her for helping Martha," Rudy said.

"Sure enough, we can look at this goat," John agreed. He started off after Rudy then stopped. "Is the goat bred already?"

"Jah, she is bred. Do you have a buck in with the ewes now?" Rudy asked.

"Jah, and we expect lambs in early March," John said.

"That will be perfect. This nanny goat will kid in March," Rudy exclaimed.

Hal followed behind the men. She felt John would take buying the goat better if he dealt with Rudy. If the goat had any problems Rudy didn't mention, John might not tease her so much if he made the choice to buy the goat.

When they entered the barn, the door banged shut, causing sharp bleats to come from a horse stall. Rudy said, "She hears our voices. Goats do not like being alone, but she would be happy with your flock. She is used to running with my sheep."

Hal noted the brown goat had a trim of white running around her face and four white stockings on her frail legs. "What breed is she?"

"Toggenburg. Her name is Gano," Rudy said.

Hal stared at the goat. "That is an odd name."

"Jah, that it is, but if you dislike it you can change the name," Rudy stated, not willing to elaborate on the origin.

"Can I go in the stall with her?" Hal asked as she watched

the goat pace along the back wall.

Rudy opened the door. "Go recht in. I milked her this year, so she is already trained to stand still. She is calmer than she looks."

Hal held her hand out to pat the goat. "Hello, Gano. I'm Hal."

Gano ran to the far corner and watched her through wide, dark brown eyes. With no where else to run, she let Hal walk up to her. When Hal put her hand on the goat's head, Gano ducked her head as if Hal hit her.

"She does not act very friendly," John stated bluntly.

"She just does not know what to make of all the strangers. After she gets used to you, she will be a pest," Rudy assured him.

"All recht, I will buy her. Jim, you want to hold on to the goat while I drive home?" John asked.

"I think I can handle that," Jim said, grinning.

Rudy led the goat to the buggy with a rope around her neck. Jim climbed in and sat at the back of the buggy. Rudy and John lifted the squalling and kicking goat. Jim grabbed the rope around the goat's neck and pulled her to him. She eyed Nora and Hal when they sat down. Her nose wrinkled up as she sniffed their direction.

When they arrived home, John drove over by his barn and stopped. Aunt Tootie had Redbird and Beth by the hands, coming to see the latest animal. Hal picked up Redbird and Nora picked up Beth.

Once Gano's hooves hit the ground, she only had Jim holding onto her rope. She bucked and strained, trying to get away. Jim held on tight and settled her down. Both girls held out a hand, wanting to pet the nanny.

Aunt Tootie gasped and sidestepped close to Nora.

"For Heaven's sake, Tootie, don't crowd me so," Nora complained.

Aunt Tootie huffed, "Sorry, but I was afraid that goat would butt me."

Jim relaxed his hold on the rope while he picked at the

girls. Gano quickly stretched her neck and got a mouth full of Aunt Tootie's skirt. The goat tugged to bring it closer to her. Aunt Tootie's face blanched as she jerked the skirt out of the goat's mouth. "Shoo, goat! Jim, hang onto her better."

"I'm sorry about that, Tootie. She just wants to say hello. She won't hurt you," Jim defended.

John decided, "Jim, let's put the goat in a pen for the night. It will easier to watch her in the day light to see how she gets along with the sheep."

"John," Aunt Tootie said. "The veterinarian stopped by this morning and said the test on the skunk came back all right. The dog can be turned loose now."

"That is voonderball gute news," Noah cried. "We can take Biscuit coon hunting now."

"I will turn him out of the shed," Daniel said as he ran that direction.

After milking, the barn went silent. Gano cried from the minute the men left the barn and continued to protest all evening.

Finally, Noah offered to go see about her. He came back to the house and related he thought she was just lonesome. Half an hour later, the goat's crying started again. This time she sounded stressed. Daniel offered to take a turn to see about the goat. After Daniel left, the goat became quiet.

When Daniel returned, Hal asked, "What did you do to make her shut up?"

"The goat tried to jump over the pen. She caught one of her back legs between the top two boards. I got her loose and gave her more hay."

Hal looked worried. "Is she all recht?"

"She's limping a little. The hair is off just above the hoof, but she will be all recht," Daniel reported.

"If only she'd settle down. The constant crying is getting on all our nerves," Hal said.

Jim patted Hal's arm. "It's like Rudy Briskey said. When she has the ewes for company, she'll be content then."

"If I recall recht, what Rudy said was once the goat gets

69

used to us she will be a pest. She is that already," John said dryly.

"Sure enough, but she was eating hay when I left. Maybe she will bed down for the night now that it is dark," Daniel said hopefully.

"Speaking of settling down, how long are we leaving Tom in the barn. He is getting restless and mad at us. The goat's bawling is bothering him, too. He just chased me out of the barn," Daniel said.

"Really?" Hal asked. "Maybe tomorrow let's turn Tom out. We'll see how he gets along with the rooster. If Tom is still mean, we'll just have to pen him up again."

Tootie's lower lip pushed out in a pout. "As mean as that rooster is, if I were you boys I'd worry about Tom's welfare if they get in a fight."

At bedtime, Hal threw her nightgown on the bed and paused to listen. "It seems peaceful in the barn yet. Daniel was recht about the goat settling down after dark."

John untied his farmer shoes and toed the heel of one. It plunked to the floor. He reached down and slid the other off. "I am glad for the peace."

A series of frantic baas broke the silence. Tom joined in, gobbling loud and hostile.

"Fudge! I spoke too soon," groaned Hal, throwing her gown back on the bed.

"So much for peace and quiet. Tom is giving the goat a hard time now that he thinks he owns the barn," John said, reaching for one of his shoes.

"Nah, John, you go on to bed. She's my goat. I'll go rescue her from Tom," Hal said.

"It might be more than you can handle. Tom is a real fighter when he is mad," John reminded her.

"Nonsense, he'll mind me," Hal said, starting for the door.

"Wait, Hal! I do not know if you should be out alone after dark," John worried.

"Don't be silly. What can happen to me between the house and the barn."

70

"That may be something Chicken Plucker might have said until recently," John declared.

"Oh, I see, but I wanted the goat so I should tend to her. You have to get up early. Now it's your turn to stop worrying and go to bed," Hal declared. "I'll be recht back."

She took a lantern off a nail in the mud room and got a match from the box behind the cookstove. She stepped out on the front porch before she lit the lantern.

Usually, the sky held a moon and a jillion stars. Just her luck, she had to be out in the dark alone with a dense fog setting in. It was cool and drizzly damp, but she didn't see the need to go back for a jacket. She wouldn't be gone that long. She'd shut Tom in the feed room for the night to keep him away from the goat and be back to the house in a few minutes.

Biscuit came from under the porch swing and nudged her bare leg with his cold nose. Hal flinched before she realized what was going on. She leaned over to rub the dog's head. "You can't sleep, either? Sorry Gano and Tom have to make such a racket."

Nothing had changed yet. The goat still sounded stressed, and Tom still gobbled angrily. That turkey was one stubborn bird. The argument wasn't going to stop any time soon without some intervention.

With Biscuit behind her, Hal hustled to the barn, holding the lantern high so she could see her surroundings. She wouldn't have thought about being fearful before John reminded her about the fires. She wouldn't admit it to him, but now that he put the idea in her head, she was nervous about being outside alone with an arsonist prowling around the country side.

A horse nickered behind the barn, and another one answered back. Hal wondered what had the horses attention. She stopped to listen. Might have been Buttercat out mousing, or a wild animal looking for a stray chicken that roosted out.

The familiar scents of hay, cows and horseflesh filled Hal's nose when she opened the barn door and stepped in. Biscuit whined. "You stay put. This is no place for you. Tom won't like

71

you any better than he does the goat."

Biscuit dropped and put his head on his front legs to wait.

Hal held the lantern high. Tom had the goat cornered at the end of the pens. She had to raise her voice to be heard as she hung the lantern on a nail. "Stop that right now, Tom!"

Tom turned to look her direction. Gano slipped past him and ran to meet her. Tom fanned his feathers out and made hissing sounds as he stomped his feet.

"Calm down, Tom. You behave yourself, and I'll let you out of here tomorrow. Stop being mean to the newcomer. You're scaring her," Hal scolded, but she stayed on the far side the goat to lead her to the pen. "Gano, you stay put. You're already limping. Don't jump over the pen and get hurt again."

Hal picked up an arm load of what had been a bale of hay. The goat must have been out for some time to fluff up the bale that much. No wonder she'd been quiet until Tom found her out of the pen.

Gano couldn't be very hungry after tearing up the bale to munch on it. Hopefully, a pile of fresh hay would keep her occupied in her pen for a few minutes. Maybe long enough for Tom to forget about the goat, and her to get to sleep.

Hal looked for Tom, wanting to make sure he wasn't going to come at her as she crossed to room to get the lantern. Her thought about trying to convince him to go in the feed room had changed. That turkey wasn't in sight. Hal mumbled, "Fine, he's gone off to sulk now that I've spoiled his fun. I can get out of here."

The back barn door to the milk room swung open slowly so the hinges wouldn't squeak. A dark form, biding time in the barn yard, stepped into the milk room. Standing very still, the person listened to Hal's scolding voice in the other room.

How lucky can I get? A foggy night that will conceal me while I burn the Lapp barn. Now I find the English redhead is in the barn recht now. That is perfect.

Edging along the wall, the dark form stopped by the milk room door to the pens. The arsonist curled fingers around the

72

handle of a scoop shovel, leaning against the wall and peeked around the door frame.

Hal took for the lantern off the nail and started to leave. From behind, she felt something hard slammed against her head. Violent pain seared through her skull. The room went swimmingly black as she lost the grip on the lantern. Hal felt herself sinking to the hard cold floor before she lost consciousness.

The intruder picked up the lantern, took the cap off the tank and tossed the lantern into the messed up hay bale. A match, swiped across a nail head in the beam behind the hay, burst into flames. The arsonist dropped the match in the fuel soaked hay. Flames licked high immediately and spread through the fluffy, dry hay.

The arsonist limped back through the milk room, moving slower than in days gone by. Dragging the wounded leg made scratchy, shuffling noises on the concrete floor. The pain grew more intense with each movement of the sore leg. Leaning on the scoop shovel that had flattened Nurse Hal was a necessity.

There now, this will just look like an accident. It will be told by all Nurse Hal met her death in her own barn, settling a fight between her goat and her turkey.

In the far dark corner of the milk room, the turkey came out of his roosting stupor. His head went up at the strange sounds of step, slide, step, slide. He sighted in on the dark shadow which was larger than the goat and didn't like what he saw or heard. He rose to his feet, lowered his head and rushed the strange sounding human that was invading his territory.

It came as a surprise to the arsonist when the dragging leg was hit full force by the large turkey. The blow caused the surprised grunt to be loud. The arsonist staggered sideways and landed forcefully against the barn wall.

With victorious gobbles much like war whoops, the turkey stuck his claws through the trousers and into the wounded leg again while he pecked hard.

More grunting and cries of pain came from the victim of Tom's flogging. The scoop shovel became a weapon again as the arsonist raised it above the turkey. The shovel smacked down hard on Tom, and the turkey sank into a feathered heap on the milk room floor. The wobbling arsonist scrambled out the back door, using the scoop shovel as a cane to stay steady.

The nervous cows and horses sniffed and snorted at the sight of a stranger. Their nervousness turned into fright. The bellowing cows kicked up a cloud of dust as they rushed off. The horses bucked and nickered as they mingled together and pushed each other in a circle.

Biscuit smelled the smoke as it billowed out around the door. He let go with his best coon treeing howl. The milk goat bleated and coughed as she filled up with smoke. When the cattle mooed, and the horses whinnied as they tromped back and forth behind the barn, Biscuit raced along the outside fence by the barn, yapping.

Noah and Daniel slipped their trousers on and woke up John.

Noah said, "Daed, something is wrong at the barn?"

Daniel saw the empty side of the bed and panicked. "Where is Mama Hal?"

"She must be in the barn yet," John cried as he leaped out of bed to dress.

The boys took the stairs two at a time and rushed for the door. On the porch, they smelled smoke and saw the flicker of flames through the barn window.

Daniel hollered back in the house, "The barn is on fire."

He rushed to the barn. Noah headed to the back barn yard.

John was at the front door when Jim and Nora came to the head of the stairs.

"What can we do to help?" Nora said.

"Use your phone to call the fire department," John ordered. "We've got to hurry, Jim. Hal went to check on her goat. She is in the barn."

Aunt Tootie burst from the clinic with her nightcap cocked on her head over one eye. "What do we do? What do we do?"

"Calm down, Tootie. I'm calling the fire department now,"

Nora said as she poked the buttons.

The men made it to the open barn door with smoke billowing around it just after Daniel went inside. Noah jumped the fence and let the scared livestock out into the pasture. He heard the racing hooves of a horse in the distance and squinted to see across the pasture. He was sure a rider just left, but because of the fog, he couldn't see as far as he could hear the sounds.

Jim ran behind the house to pump buckets of water while John stepped in the barn. Daniel came to meet him with Hal in his arms.

"Hal," John shouted.

"Mama Hal is alive but not awake. She is full of smoke," Daniel said, coughing. "I will take her to the clinic."

Jim arrived with two buckets of water. He'd left Nora pumping more. Aunt Tootie came across the yard with two more buckets. As John took one bucket, he said, "Aendi Tootie, will you go tend to Hal? She is hurt. Have Nora call the ambulance."

The men waded through the smoke to throw water on the flames. The fire was burning the horse stall wall above the bale. Noah brought filled buckets and threw water on the fire.

The goat was bawling frantically as she raced around her pen.

"Get the goat out of here, Noah," John said. "Tom, too."

Noah opened the pen door and grabbed the milk goat by the neck. He held onto her to keep her from balking as they passed the fire. It didn't take much to shoo her outside when she smelled the cooler air.

Noah searched for Tom but didn't find him. The back milk room door was open which it wasn't supposed to be. Maybe Tom went in there to get away from the fire. He was smart enough to fly over the back door half door.

They formed a bucket brigade up until they heard the fire trucks coming. Biscuit set up a howl as the firemen pulled their hoses into the barn and doused the flames. Daniel wrapped his arms around the dog's neck. As he pulled Biscuit away from the barn, the dog dragged all four feet.

The excitement was too much for the goat. Gano left her hiding spot in the lean to and raced passed Biscuit, looking for a safer place to hide. The dog wrestled out of Daniel's arms and raced after her. Daniel let him go. At least, the two of them would be be out of the way.

The ambulance pulled in behind the fire truck. Aunt Tootie paced back and forth on the porch, waiting for the three paramedics to get to her. "Over here," she cried as she opened the clinic door for them and the gurney.

Aunt Tootie led the medical personnel to the bed. They took in the situation with a practiced eye.

"What happened to her?" Daryl asked Aunt Tootie.

"I don't know. Daniel carried Hallie in here from the barn, and she was unconscious. She hasn't woke up yet."

Hal moved slightly at the sound of familiar voices.

"Nurse Hal, it's Daryl. How you doing?" His demeanor was serious as he studied and assessed her.

"My head hurts," she said weakly.

Daryl knelt beside the bed and put his hand under Hal's neck to lift her up. He saw a swollen lump with a gash running through it on the back of her head.

Steve took her vital signs. "Blood pressure and pulse on the low side."

"We'll put oxygen on her. Hal, you hang in there. We have to lift you up to the gurney. As fast as the ambulance can go, we'll get you to the hospital to be checked out," Daryl said, patting her shoulder as Ivan and Steve rolled the gurney beside the bed.

The three paramedics lifted the sheet under Hal and hoisted her on the gurney. The quick movement was painful. Hal passed out again. The attendants rushed her down the steps and to the ambulance.

John called from beside the barn, "How is she?"

Daryl said, "We can't be sure. Hal has an abrasion on the back of her head. Looks like someone hit her from behind."

Nora said, "I'm going with her, John. You come when you can."

With the siren blasting, Daryl headed for the hospital with Nora in the front seat beside him. As soon as the ambulance pulled out on the road, another fire truck pulled in and parked by the house. The two firemen climbed out of their truck and walked over by the barn. One of them called in the door to the chief to see if they were needed.

As soon as the firemen thought the burn area was wet enough they turned off the hoses. Fire Chief Charlie Miller came to where John and the others stood in the house yard.

"We've got the fire out. You're lucky you didn't lose your barn like Mr. Stolfus did," Charlie said.

"That is for sure," John agreed.

"I take it the phone shed was still all right when you made the call about the fire?" The fire chief asked.

John looked puzzled. "We did not use the phone shed. My mother- in-law has a cell phone. She called from here."

"I see. The last fire truck that just pulled in had to stop and hose down a fire in the phone shed," Chief Miller said. "The guy sure had a busy night this time, lighting his fires. We found the remnants of a lantern on burnt hay ashes inside the barn. The fuel from the lantern helped spread the fire."

"Jah, Hal took a lantern with her to see in the barn to check a new goat she bought," John explained.

"Where was Mrs. Lapp when you found her?" The chief turned to Daniel when he spoke.

"Over by the wall where she would have hung the lantern."

"The medic said she was hit on the head," John said.

"Quite a distance between the fire and where Hal was found, don't you think, Chief?" Jim asked.

"My guess is someone wanted the fire to look like an accident. With Nurse Hal out cold, we'd find the lantern and her after it was too late," the chief said.

"Sure enough, someone else had been in the barn. I heard a

horse gallop across the pasture, but I could not see anything for the fog. I do know it was not one of our horses. I was just turning them loose," Noah said.

"If it is safe to leave now, we need to go to the hospital to see how bad hurt my wife is hurt," John said. "I want to be with her."

"Go ahead. We'll watch the barn for a while yet. We're going to fork some of that smoldering hay and pitch it out the back door. I'll notify the sheriff when we get back to town to come look around in the morning so don't move the lantern or anything else," the chief cautioned.

Chapter 7

Jim drove his car to the hospital. Smoke had settled on them and soaked into their clothes, but none of them wanted to take the time to clean up. Hal's family rushed through the hospital emergency doors and stopped at the nurse's station.

The night nurse came down the hall to them. "You related to Nurse Hal?"

"Jah, I am her husband. These are her sons and father," John said. "How is she?"

"Awake, but she has a whale of a headache. Mr. Lapp, you can go see her." She pointed to the waiting room. "The rest of you go in that room. I'll send Nurse Hal's mother to talk to you."

John walked briskly down the ER hall with the nurse. "Nurse Hal has a concussion. She'll have to take it easy for a few days and stay in bed. She'll be dizzy if she tries to get up and might fall. Going to the bathroom will be about it until she sees the doctor again."

"Sure enough," John said. "We will take gute care of her."

Hal was dozing when they entered the exam room. Nora rose from her chair and came to them. She said softly, "Hal went to sleep a few minutes ago. She has a bad headache. Resting is the best thing for her."

The nurse asked Nora, "You want to go out to the waiting

room and talk to the worried men waiting for news?"

Nora looked at John. "Jim and the boys came with me. Aendi Tootie stayed with the girls."

"Tell them the doctor said Nurse Hal will be fine after she rests," the nurse said to Nora. "She will be moved to a room soon. After the doctor makes rounds in the morning, he'll probably release her."

John spent a few minutes watching Hal sleep. Satisfied she was resting all right, he walked to the waiting room. "We might as well go home now."

When they arrived back at the house, Nora went into the clinic to wake up Aunt Tootie to tell her Hal would be home in the morning. Aunt Tootie had the girls behind her in bed. They were sleeping soundly. Nora debated waking Aunt Tootie and decided to wait to talk to her until morning. She didn't want to wake the little girls. They might have trouble going back to sleep.

John wasn't sure any of the rest of them could rest easy after such an unsettling night, but he was sound asleep the minute his head hit the pillow.

The next morning as soon as breakfast, devotion and the chores were done, John sent Noah to Emma's school to tell her what happened to Hal.

Jim and Nora took John to the hospital to pick up Hal. Doctor Christensen said she was to have bed rest for two days. Her equilibrium might be off for at least that long from such a hard blow to the head. After two days, Hal should come back for a checkup before he'd release her to go back to her regular routine.

Back home, John helped Hal out of the back seat. He put his arm around her waist to help her up the steps and into the house. She headed him toward the couch and eased on to it.

Nora scolded "That won't do, Hal. You heard the doctor's orders. You're to lie down."

Aunt Tootie clucked like a setting hen. "Home a whole minute, and she's not minding right away."

"One thing I'm not doing is get stuck in my bed upstairs like I was the last time I had a concussion. I want to be down here with my family," Hal demanded as she laid her head on the back of the couch.

"All right, I'm going upstairs to get your pillow and a quilt to cover up with. If you're staying down here, you're going to stretch out on that couch," Nora insisted as she headed for the stairs.

"Don't take a quilt off the bed. John will need the cover. Get one out of the quilt chest sitting by the window. There's plenty of quilts in it," Hal said.

John backed up beside Jim while Nora and Aunt Tootie scolded Hal. After the matter of her resting on the couch was settled, he put his hand over Hal's and squeezed. "Now that you are all settled in, I want to look around in the barn again. Charlie Miller and Sheriff Dawson will be here soon to check the barn, then we can clean the mess up."

"See you later," Hal said with a weak wave.

Aunt Tootie kept watch at the living room window. Just before eleven, she announced the sheriff and fire chief had arrived. Half and hour later, she related the sheriff and fire chief were headed to the house.

Aunt Tootie opened the door.

"Morning, ma'am," the sheriff said. "Would it be possible to talk to Nurse Hal a minute?"

"She isn't feeling well and is supposed to stay quiet," Aunt Tootie declared.

"It's all right, Aunt Tootie. I can talk to them," Hal said.

"All right, you can come in." Aunt Tootie begrudgingly stepped out of the way.

Chief Miller nodded. "Glad you're going to be all right, Nurse Hal. You gave everyone quite a scare."

Sheriff Dawson said, "You got quite a wallop on the head I hear."

"Feels like it for sure," Hal replied.

"We won't disturb you long. We just wondered if you could tell us anything about what happened in the barn,"

81

Sheriff Dawson said.

"Not a thing. I was ready to leave. Last thing I remember I reached for the lantern and felt like my head exploded," Hal said. "Have any leads?"

"No. I hate to tell you this, but clearly, you were meant to burn in the barn. Otherwise, the arsonist would have let you go outside before he set the fire," the sheriff said. "You made anyone mad lately?"

"Nah, but maybe the arsonist was anxious to get away, and he didn't want to wait for me to leave. He might have been afraid I'd see him. He was working under cover of that dense fog. If it lifted, he might have been afraid if he waited much longer someone would see him out on the road," Hal reasoned.

"You could be right," Charlie Miller agreed. "We best get out of here and let you rest."

"Feel better soon," Sheriff Dawson said.

Noah rode in from going to the school to talk to Emma. He ran up the porch steps and stuck his head in the door. "You doing all recht, Mama Hal?"

"Jah, just a little swimmy headed yet. I can't stand up for very long, and even if I could, your mammi and aendi won't let me," Hal grumbled to him.

"I told Emma you had been in the hospital. She is going to come over to visit this afternoon," Noah said. "Now I have to get to the barn and help."

When John, Jim and the boys came in for lunch, they were blackened by soot and ashes.

Hal opened her eyes when they banged the screen door.

Redbird and Beth frowned from the quilt on the floor where they were playing with a set of toy dishes.

Redbird scolded, "Shhh! Mama sleep."

"Sorry, Redbird," John said quietly. He turned to Jim, nodding at Redbird as he grinned. "I think we have another Emma on our hands."

Hal rolled over toward them, rubbing the sleep out of her eyes. "John, how you coming with clean up?"

82

"Gute, it won't take much longer. The fire was put out before it could do much damage."

Hal gasped. "I forgot to ask. How's my milk goat?"

"Jumping out of the pen this morning more times than we could count," Noah commented.

"Sure enough, she followed us around while we cleaned the barn even when we did not want her to," Daniel said.

"In the way and a nuisance for sure," John summed up dryly.

"Can't Gano be put in the pasture with the sheep now? That will probably satisfy her," Hal suggested.

Noah said, "I think that is a gute idea for this afternoon. The time has come for the goat to get to know the sheep flock."

"Mama Hal, we have bad news," Daniel stated glumly. The person who hit you on the head killed Tom Turkey. He must have tried to protect you and fought with the man."

"Fudge! That's awful," Hal cried. "I am so sorry, boys. We will certainly miss Tom, ain't so?"

John said, "If we had found the turkey in time, we could have butchered him, but by this morning, he was already stiff."

"Daed, we could not eat Tom," Noah cried.

"Nah, we could not," Daniel agreed with a fast shake of his head.

"John, that was not a very gute idea," scolded Hal.

"Jah, I forgot for a moment he was everybody's pet. You might as well carry him off to the timber for the coyotes to find," John said to the boys.

Daniel's shoulders sagged. Noah's lips tightened as he stared at the floor. Hal could tell John's second plan for the deceased pet wasn't any better received than the first one. The boys didn't want to let the coyotes eat Tom.

"I have a better idea. Would you like to bury Tom in the walnut grove by Patches, say a prayer over him and put a cross on his grave?" Hal asked.

Nora listened at the kitchen doorway. "Sounds like a good idea to me. What do you think, John?"

Noah and Daniel perked up, waiting for John to agree. "If

the boys want to do that, it is all recht with me. Tom Turkey has earned his way around here as a watch dog. He deserves a nice burial for protecting Hal when the arsonist killed him. He should have a proper burial. That what you want for Tom, boys?"

"Jah," they said in unison and started for the front door.

"Tom Turkey should have a proper send off. We all got a kick out of him. Can Mammi and I come?" Jim asked.

"Sure enough," Noah said. "Come on, Daniel. We'll get the shovel."

"Wait a minute," Jim said. "I think the funeral could wait until after lunch. You might have your grandma and aunt after you with a wooden spoon if you don't eat first."

"We wish you could go with us, Mama Hal," Daniel said.

"I wish I could, too," Hal replied wistfully.

"Oh, no, she's not getting up for at least another day," Nora protested.

Hal winked at Daniel. "You heard your mammi. I'll say a prayer for Tom from here and visit his grave as soon as I feel up to it."

While they milked that evening Noah said, "Daed, we are going to take the dog through the timber by Bender Creek this evening. We plan on stopping in on that party."

"Are you really sure you want to do this?" John frowned.

"We are now," Daniel said. "After what happened to Mama Hal and Tom, we want to find the fire setter as bad as everyone else does. He is dangerous."

"You're right about that, Daniel," Jim said. Your Mama Hal is lucky she survived that blow on her head and to not be burned alive with the barn. That makes me worry about you boys getting hurt by the same man if you find out who he is."

"You have to be careful," John cautioned.

"We will, Daed," Noah agreed.

After supper, Noah and Daniel put Biscuit on a leash and walked across the pasture to the timber along Bender Creek. A boom box, cranked up to the max, blasted them with music long before they arrived at the clearing.

Albert Jostle swaggered over to meet them. He shouted to be heard over the music. "I thought you said you did not want to come to the party."

Noah shook his head. "Nah, I said we had not thought about coming. We decided to run our coon dog in Bender timber to get him used to trailing again."

"We heard the music and stopped in," Daniel added.

"Come on. You might like the party well enough to hang around," Albert said loudly.

When Daniel tugged on Biscuit's rope, the dog stiffened his legs and drug his feet. He didn't want to go with them. "Come on, boy. We will not stay long," Daniel whispered in his ear.

Biscuit whined as he flopped down in the dried leaves. He put his front paws over his ears. The music hurt his ears, and he didn't want any closer.

"Tie him to a bush. We can come back to get him," Noah said.

"I cannot say I blame the dog. The music is too loud. The mood Biscuit is in he might bite someone," Daniel joked.

When they caught up with Albert, he said to the others, "Look who is here to join us."

Teenage boys and their girlfriends looked up to see who Albert was talking about.

Noah and Daniel knew the Plain part of the group. Some of the strangers were English. The ones they did know waved a greeting. That was easier than trying to speak from a distance which would be drowned out by the loud music anyway.

Albert sat down by a black haired, girl in a tank top and skinny jeans. He gave her a lascivious smile as he rubbed her thigh. "This girl's mine for the night, but I might could pry a couple of girls away from my two brothers if you want them."

Noah shook his head. "Denki, but nah. Next time, we will bring our own dates."

"What can I offer you boys to drink? The keg is over there." He wiggled a finger at a gooseberry bush with the keg by it. He picked up a half full bottle of clear liquid and said with a slur, "I have vodka here. Using orange juice in it tonight."

"We are not used to the hard stuff. Got any pop?" Noah asked.

"Sure enough, it is Rueban Rogies's night to furnish the pop in that cooler by him," Albert said, pouring vodka in a glass. He reached in a paper sack and pulled out a small bottle of Tropicana orange juice, screwed off the cap and emptied it into his glass.

Daniel grabbed the back of Noah's arm and nodded.

Noah whispered, "I see." He said to Albert, "We will go get the pop. Denki."

When they approached Rueban, he rose to his knees and took the lid off the cooler. "You looking for the pop?"

"Sure enough," Noah said, taking a mountain dew and handing Daniel one. "How much do we owe you?"

"A buck a piece," Rueban said.

Noah slipped two one dollar bills out of his trouser pocket while Daniel checked out the teenagers in the clearing. "It looks like you had a gute turn out."

"Anyone new to you show up lately?" Noah asked.

Rueban shook his head. "Nah, same old crowd all summer."

After an hour and a half of wandering from couple to couple, Noah said, "We better get back to Biscuit."

They stopped by Albert and his girlfriend long enough to say they were leaving. Noah excused he didn't want their dog to get restless. He might untie himself and run off.

Albert slurred, "I hope you had a gute time. You are wilcom to come again."

Noah stuffed his hands in his trouser pockets. "Denki, but it is not safe to be out here with that arsonist roaming around setting fires all the time."

"I do not fear that person," Albert bragged.

"That so? Why not?" Daniel asked.

Albert shrugged.

"You know who the guy is?" Noah asked.

"Nah," Albert elongated and belched. "Do you?"

"Nah, that is why he scares us," Noah said. "We will run our dog through the timber as we head for home. See you soon."

It was some time after midnight. The stars were fading, and the quarter moon sank low enough to be hidden by the tree line.

I wish I had not over slept. I meant to be home by now, but it is not much farther to the Weber Sisters house if I keep moving. Those women have to be stopped from luring English into the Plain community to eat with them. Getting close to the English gives Plain people ideas that take them away from the Ordnung. I'll set fire to the house and head for home. Wish I could move faster, but I cannot stand the pain. Not tonight.

The golden draft horse walked at an easy pace on the country road along Bender Creek. He shied sideways at the Bender timber line when he heard the throbbing sounds of the teenage party slice through the trees.

"Easy, Jack. I did not know there would be such a wicked gathering here tonight. I will change my plan to teach those that have strayed from the faith a lesson. I can get an earlier start next time to visit the Weber sisters."

Once the horse turned around in the direction he came from, his ears perked up. Alerted to the smell of kerosene spilling from juice bottles into the grass and dried leaves under the trees, he tensed. The horse realized what was to come next now that he had been through this procedure several times.

The raspy scratch of a match head ignited it into a flame when the head was rubbed against the sandpaper side of the box. A flick of the wrist landed the match in the kerosene spill. The flame flickered and took hold, spreading fire through the spill. Smoke boiled up as fire consumed the leaves and grass.

A nudge of a knee in the draft horse's ribs made him move away. A pull on the reins stopped him again for a repeat of another spill and ignited match.

The first fire was taking hold, spreading and creating a

cloud of smoke as it licked at the trees. The next fire would soon catch up.

Now I will go home.

Albert left his girl long enough to stagger past the underbrush to take a leak. He sniffed the air. As fast as he could scrambled on his leaden feet, he ran back into the clearing, crying, "Fire!". The others weren't paying any attention to him. He dived for the boom box and turned it off. "Smoke! The timber is on fire. Quick, get out of here."

Noah and Daniel heard the excitement in Albert's voice while Daniel untied the dog. They turned to see him come out of the brush and looked where he pointed.

"Odd he should see that fire right now after we talked to him about the arsonist," Noah said.

Daniel tugged on Noah's arm. "We need to get out of here. Fire will travel fast in this dry timber. We are on foot."

The teenagers jumped into action, packing and closing coolers. They were soon running for buggies, horses and cars.

Noah said, "We can head for the phone shed and call the fire department."

Albert heard him as he past the boys. "I have a cell phone. I can call." He brought a phone out of his trouser pocket and made the call as he ran.

Sirens blared when Noah and Daniel were a mile from home. They made it safely to the road before the fire ate its way through the timber.

John waited up for them on the porch swing. His voice came out of the dark. "How did it go?"

"We watched Albert Jostle spike his vodka with a small bottle of Tropicana orange juice like has been found at the other fires," Noah said. "I asked him if he had heard anything about the arsonist. I told him it did not seem like a gute idea to have a party with someone sneaking around setting fires."

"Albert said he did not worry about the arsonist. We left and stopped to untie Biscuit from a gooseberry bush near the clearing. Next thing we knew Albert yelled the timber was on fire," Daniel said.

John gasped. "What?"

"Albert came out of the bushes and told everyone to get out of the timber fast," Noah said.

"Did everyone get out all right?" John asked.

"Jah, the breeze blew the smoke at the party so they had plenty of warning," Daniel said.

"Did you call the fire department?"

"We said we would run for the phone shed. Albert Jostle said we did not have to do that. He has a cell phone," Noah shared.

"Sure enough, you think Albert set the fire?" John asked.

"We did not see him do it, Daed? All we know is, he was bragging the arsonist did not scare him, and he is the first one who saw the fire," Noah affirmed.

Chapter 8

The in between Sunday came and went quietly. Normally, the Lapp family might have gone visiting since they didn't have worship service. They, as well as everyone else in the Plain community, felt it was safer to stay home until the arsonist was caught. The next Sunday, when they had a worship service to attend, the whole Plain community would be there no matter what.

Hal was happy to spend the quiet day at home with her parents and aunt. She knew she wouldn't have them around much longer. Besides, she continued to have a nagging headache that subsided only when she remembered to take Tylenol.

Gano continued to be a headache in the making for John and the boys. The milk goat seemed to like the sheep, and the flock liked her which was a good thing. It was just that Gano liked people better. She jumped over the pasture fence as soon as she heard voices in the yard or barn. The goat was a soft footed escape artist. She'd slipped up on members of the family and bit into their shirt or apron. The goat pulled backward before they knew she was close, almost knocking them off their feet.

Aunt Tootie had just about quit going outside by herself. Between the rooster bristling up at everyone and the goat trailing them, she decided it was safer to be house bound.

On Monday morning, John decided to donate a load of hay bales so early that morning, Jim and he dropped bales from the loft to Noah and Daniel on a hay wagon. John climbed on top a stack of bales that reached to the rafter and handed the bales down to Jim. John's foot sank into a hole between the bales. To keep from falling, he grabbed the rafter. His fingers pushed something off in front of him, and it landed by his feet. John picked the radio up and stared at it.

"What you got?" Jim asked.

"A radio," John answered, holding it up.

Jim asked, "How do you reckon it got up there?"

"I do not know," John said solemnly. "This could only be hidden by one or both of my sons. Both of them know this radio is not permitted by our Ordnung."

From the wagon, David called, "Are you having trouble in the loft?"

Jim went to the window. "No, this old man just needed a rest. Another bale will be down quick like." He balanced on the bales as he walked back to John. "We should keep the bales coming."

"Jah, I will worry about this problem later. Jim, keep this to yourself about me finding this radio. It is just going to mysteriously disappear for right now," John grinned.

"I understand," Jim said, returning the grin.

That afternoon, the boys took turns staying with their pumpkins and squashes in the stand and taking the goat back to the pasture. Gano figured out where they were in a hurry and could be counted on to show up several times a day to say hello.

After supper, Daniel complained to Hal that he spent most of his day taking the goat back to the pasture.

John replied, "We now know why Rudy had the goat in that horse stall in his barn. It was the only place with high enough walls the goat could not jump over. If we had not showed up when we did, he would have sold that nuisance goat at the salebarn."

91

"Wonder how Rudy Briskey came to name the goat Gano?" Jim puzzled. "Sure is a funny name for a goat."

"It is for sure, Dad," Hal said. "John, does Gano mean something in Pennsylvania Dutch?"

John shook his head. "Nah."

Aunt Tootie piped up. "It sounds like a Spanish word."

"You might be right," Nora agreed. "Hal, do you still have that book on language translations to English we gave you when you became a nurse."

"Jah, it's in the quilt chest in our bedroom. I'll go get it," Hal said and went upstairs.

She came back and sat by the gas lamp at the end of the cough to look through it. "Let's see. Here is the Spanish section." She went through the G pages." "Oh, no!"

"What does it say for Gano, dear?" Aunt Tootie asked.

With a meek tone, Hal said, "Gano means I win."

John grimaced. "Are you sure?"

"Jah," Hal said.

"That means in Rudy Briskey language that he got the last laugh on us again," John grumbled. He rubbed his forehead and fingered his bible for a moment. Suddenly, his face lightened up, and he burst out laughing.

Just the reaction the rest of them hoped for from John, since they were having a hard time holding back their laughter.

A few minutes after that, Bishop Bontrager and his wife, Jane, stopped by to see how Hal was feeling. While they sat at the kitchen table drinking coffee and eating a piece of spice cake, John asked how the plans for the barn raising were coming along.

Bishop Bontrager tapped his cup with his fingers. "In the previous week, volunteer help to build the barn had been secured by a committee that mailed invitations to other nearby Amish communities. Also, offers of help came through the Amish hot line."

"Exactly what is that?" Jim asked.

Jane explained, "We have a telephone call list that enables members to quickly forward news, prayer requests and important church news."

The bishop added, "The committee in charge of notifying everyone about the barn raising gave them two days notice on the hot line. A week's notice was provided for Stolfus relatives farther away that will want to help."

"Levi Yoder stopped by our stand," Noah said. "He says the Amish sawmill had been turning out oak and pine planks, laboring fast to fill the order in time for the barn raising."

"Sure seems like an old fashion event, putting up a barn in this day and age this way," Nora surmised.

Hal nodded. "Barn raisings are associated with the Amish, but if I remember my American history right in the 1700 and 1800's during homesteading, barn raising events united English neighbors regardless of religious affiliation. Volunteers provided labor for residents who lost a barn through disaster or who wanted to expand their farming."

Jim added, "The tradition of building raising is part of the past as far as the English are concerned. As time passed, the English invented labor saving devices like cranes which reduced the need for volunteers to do the heavy lifting.

A crane is rented to use to set center beams and complete other heavy chores like lifting the walls. Less accidents happened when a crane lifts the heavy beams and walls instead of many men working together. Construction on a building gets done just as fast.

Now English people are willing to pay carpenters to build houses and barns."

"The Amish see the tradition of barn raising differently, ain't so, Bishop?" John raised an eyebrow at Elton Bontrager. "Plain people don't expect barn or house raisings to ever go away. Helping each other is part of being Amish."

After the Bontragers said good bye, John followed Elton and Jane outside. He shoved his hands in his trouser pockets as he spoke, "Bishop, could I talk to you for a minute in private?"

"Sure enough. Jane, go on to the buggy," Elton said and watched for his wife to get out of ear shot. "Now, John, was ist letz?"

"Today we filled a wagon with hay to take over to the new Stolfus barn when it is done. While Jim and I worked in the hayloft, I accidentally discovered a transistor radio on a rafter."

Bishop Elton clasped his hands in front of him. "I see. Do you know the owner?"

"Nah, but I wondered if you might consider a sermon on our beliefs about no modern conveniences, and aim it at at the youth in rumspringa. Perhaps, it will be what Noah or Daniel or both of them needs to hear to repent for buying the radio."

"Be glad to help you out, Brother John. This sounds like a timely sermon that might help other youth to give up the English ways," the bishop said. "If the sermon works, let me know how this matter turned out."

"Denki, you can count on that, Bishop," John said.

The Stolfus barn raising was actually a thoroughly planned process. At the beginning, Plain children descended on the Stolfus farm with their sleeves rolled up, ready to start and finish the clean up effort in a day. Removing the old barn's foundation, rubble and ashes was necessary. A very long labor intensive day, but young and enthusiastic hands made light work. While children cleared the cement blocks away, they salvaged the usable blocks to use in the new foundation.

The school children of all ages chattered as they worked and even broke out in a hymn. At midday, they stopped for lunch when women called them to take a break.

Hal, her mother, and aunt brought sandwiches. Linda Yoder and her mother-in-law, Margaret, brought potato salad. Emma brought a pea salad. Edna Stolfus baked three cakes. Roseanna Nisely made one hundred doughnuts. The drinks in coolers were grape Kool Aid and ice tea. Several coolers of water were for any time the youngsters were thirsty. Some just needed to wash down the bad taste from the smoke and ashes.

Eager to get finished by the end of the day, the children ate and returned to work. The women were packing up their baskets and washing dishes when they heard the painful yell. They stopped to look toward what remained of the rubble. The children had grouped together, milling around Mark Yoder.

Linda Yoder exclaimed, "Something is wrong with my son. He's hopping on one foot."

The women ran to the boy, Daniel's age, as he hopped across the driveway with his brother, Levi, and Noah holding him upright. Daniel and Davie Stolfus got behind Mark and helped lower him to the lawn.

The boy held his left foot, rocking back and forth as he groaned.

"What happened, Mark?" Linda asked, pushing his dark hair back from his sweaty forehead.

Mark swallowed hard to hold back tears. "I stepped on a nail. It went through my shoe."

Hal went to her knees beside him. "Let me see. She looked at the sole of his farmer shoe. The head of a square, rusty nail stuck out an inch from the sole. The rest was in Mark's foot.

"Bring me a bolt cutter to take off the head of the nail so we can slip Mark's shoe off. We'll also need a pair of pliers to pull the nail out of his foot," Hal said.

"I'll get them," Davie shuffled away, headed for the tool shed.

Mark's completion was ashen. Hal was afraid he'd pass out. "Linda, sit beside Mark and hold his hand."

"What can we do?" Edna asked.

"I need a pan of water, a cloth and towel. We have to wash the blood off Mark's foot so I can see to clean the wound. Also, clean cloth to use as a bandage," Hal listed.

Edna Stolfus and Margaret Yoder rushed to the house. Davie came back with the bolt cutter.

Levi Yoder took the cutter from Davie. "Let me cut the nail off, Nurse Hal."

"Gute. Noah, hold Mark's leg gute and tight so he doesn't flinch." As Noah moved by Mark, a glance at the concern on Daniel's face for his best friend told Hal he needed something to do to help. "Daniel, you put your arm around Mark and lower him to the ground. Stay by his side to keep him from moving. All recht, Noah, hold the foot steady. Levi, cut the nail head."

Levi put the end of the nail cutter against Mark's shoe sole and snapped the nail head off swiftly. He got back out of the way and handed the bolt cutter to Davie to take back to the shed.

"Now I'll untie the shoe and ease it off his foot. All of you be prepared for the sight of blood," Hal warned. She loosened the shoe string, took it out of the eyes and pulled the tongue back toward the shoe toe. "Hold tight, Noah," Hal said softly as she eased the shoe off with one smooth movement.

"Mama Hal, Mark fainted," Daniel cried.

"That's gute. We'll clean the wound before he wakes up," Hal said.

Emma knelt beside Hal. Edna handed her the pan of warm water. Margaret set a basket with bandaging material near Hal and laid a cloth and towel on top the basket. Emma dropped the cloth in the wash pan.

Hal rolled the black sock off Mark's foot as blood dripped from it. "Denki, ladies." The sock resisted on top the foot. Hal eased the sock up and found the nail had gone through to the top of the foot.

"What else can we do to help?" Edna asked.

"Pray," Hal replied. As she studied the nail, with blood oozing around it, in the bottom of Mark's foot, the women circled around them and knelt to pray. "Noah, hold his leg tight at the ankle." Hal picked up the pliers and got a good bite on the nail shank. She gave a pull, and the nail came out. Blood poured from the wound.

Emma handed Hal the wash cloth.

Hal wiped as much blood as she could from the site. "I believe the nail hit an a vein. We need to send Mark to the hospital. Someone call the ambulance."

Davie Stolfus shuffled off to the phone booth without being told.

Emma rinsed out the wash cloth. Hal wrapped it around Mark's foot and pressed in on the wound sites, hoping pressure would slow the bleeding.

96

It seemed to take forever before the ambulance stopped by the group in the yard. Daryl and Ivan wheeled the gurney over while Steve carried the back board.

Steve asked Linda Yoder for Mark's name and age with history of medicines and allergies. Daryl asked Hal for an assessment of the wound as Ivan and he rolled the gurney to the ambulance. In a matter of minutes, the ambulance raced down the road hidden in plumes of dust.

On Tuesday, three men were placed in charge of constructing the barn - a contractor, a mason and a post-and-beam expert. They coordinated teams of workers for the project. Over a hundred men worked each day. That meant almost as many women came to cook, and a great number of children did odd jobs.

The barn raising started with the foundation. A small group of men mortared cement blocks together. True to his word, Chicken Plucker and his sons had taken out the barn yard fence and laid out the area for the new foundation farther away from the house. By late afternoon the foundation was together and drying.

The following day, Wednesday, the early morning sun shone brightly over harvested corn and hay fields. Timbers revealed a patchwork of colored leaves. A heavy frost coated everything, lending gay sparkles to the landscape.

Over two hundred Amish men, women, and a countless number of children, walked the rural roads. Some took short cuts as they traversed harvested fields. Others drove steeled wheeled, blue or green tractors, buggies and horses. They started arriving around eight that morning.

Boys met buggies at the entrance of the hay field behind the house. They took charge of the buggies and tied up the horses to the ropes stretched out from hay wagon to hay wagon. The field quickly filled with neat rows of buggies.

The men gathered at the site of the barn's foundation. Lumber, boxes of nails and stacks of roofing tin were neatly piles, ready to be assembled by workers during the frolic. The

97

smell of fresh cut wood lingered over the area.

When it looked like all the crew was assembled, Bishop Bontrager came to stand by the barn foundation and motioned for the Plain people to mill around him. He held his hand up for quiet. "We shall have the dedication for the barn raising now."

The men took off their straw hats. Everyone bowed their heads, and the children quieted down. Bishop Bontrager raised his voice to be heard by the large crowd. "The Lord will work among us with the unfolding of this barn. This is His way to make gute things come from bad if we let Him. Prayers, support and counsel from all of you, our brothers, sisters and friends are solicited for our safety as this barn goes up.

May your lives bear witness to the message of hard work and fellowship we are called to share by putting up this barn. For the Lord is present with us, His people. He celebrates life with us. This barn we dedicate today is already yours, O God, for you are our God! We are the sheep of your pasture, a flock under your care. Keep our workers safe this day. Praise be to God! Amen and Amen." He raised his head and put his straw hat back on. "Now, builders, we can begin already."

Abel Beiler supervised the completion of the work. He had many years of experience in such endeavors. The workers participated under his direction to erect the frame, walls, and the roof.

After a short discussion with the contractors, the men rolled up their sleeves and went to work at the various jobs. The older, experienced men acted as supervisors. Men and teenage boys cut boards to fit. Others nailed the boards together. Young boys ran errands, carried tools where needed and kept the men's nail aprons filled.

Early that morning, the operator parked the crane off to the side. With his hard hat on, the man picked up a hammer and pounded nails while he waited for a signal to bring the crane forward and get hooked up to a beam or wall.

The women and girls prepared for the noon feast as they visited. Hal still have a slight headache. She didn't know if she could stay on her feet all day or not. She probably should have stayed home after the stress of the day before, but she didn't want to miss the barn raising.

What a trooper Mark Yoder was, He insisted on coming. Right now he sat under the maple shade tree in the Stolfus yard with his bandaged foot elevated on a rolled quilt. From the frown on the boy's face, Hal figured his foot was throbbing, but he didn't want to stay home and miss out on the barn raising. If Mark could endure suffering from his aching foot to be there, she could put up with a slight headache.

This was a special day her parents and aunt would have to tell their friends about when they went home. Nora was helping Margaret Yoder peel potatoes. They talked about how nice the fall weather had been. Margaret said God blessed them with this beautiful weather for the barn raising.

Aunt Tootie helped Eli Mast's mother, Edna, unpack the crates containing the table settings. They chatted as if they had been life long friends. Hal smiled. *Why not? The two elderly women are very much alike.*

Silver haired Edna, with burnished skin from working outside all her life, was a complainer about everyone's imperfections and her own health. Hal learned long ago not to ask Edna how she was feeling. Not if she didn't want to listen to a vast list of the woman's ailments.

At the moment, Aunt Tootie was at the top of her element. She was in the middle of explaining to Edna about the skunk and how the smell almost choked her to death. Edna hung on to every word with a sympathetic look.

Jim, somewhere among the men, pounded nails and enjoyed every minute of it. Hal felt a deep gratitude to the Plain people for accepting her family among them while they vacationed with her.

Many of the dishes had been prepared ahead of time. The women decided what dish to bring so there would be plenty to eat.

Roseanna Nisely asked her daughter, Ella Miller, to squeeze lemons and prepare coolers full of lemonade to go with the meal. Other coolers held water and tea.

The toddlers had been taken to the house yard. They lay on blankets, taking a nap or sit quietly as they watch the men work. Katie Yost watched over them to keep them out of the way. On one quilt laid babies, napping.

Younger teenage boys took benches from the bench wagon and set up tables and benches in the hay field for the meal.

For the younger generation of boys and girls, this was a learning experience so they would know how to work at a barn raising when it was their turn to be in charge.

The operator ribbed up the crane and lifted the frame work for each side of the barn while the men hammered the frames in place. Soon the frames of the barn were secured.

More than just a construction project, the beautiful fall day provided a community gathering. Families attended for fellowship as well as to help the Stolfus family. Hearing laughter and chatter around her reminded Hal of cheerful bird songs. However, the workers pounding nails and others making saws grate through wood added to her headache.

Homemade bread filled the air with a delicious aroma as young girls helped Aunt Tootie and Edna Mast set the table. Other women set bowls of food in the middle of the tables. A couple of young boys were sent to tell the first shift of hard working men it was time to stop for lunch. Those men took in the good smells as they brought their appetite to the table with them.

Chapter 9

Lunch was served in two shifts for the men and boys to accommodate work schedules. While some ate, others worked to keep the construction going. Admittedly, lunch took longer than planned, as people welcomed the chance to catch up on news.

While the men sat down for first lunch Rudy Briskey's booming voice told those nearest him at his table, "Have you heard my corn field was set on fire. I lost all my shocks."

"Did you see anyone around?" Eli Mast asked.

"Nah, it was the noise of the frightened sheep and the dog that woke me up."

"What did you do?" Cooner Jonas Rogies asked.

"I called the fire department. The firemen were able to put the fire out just before it entered my house yard. The whole field was destroyed," Rudy lamented.

Bishop Bontrager said, "That is quite a loss. If you need winter feed, bring it up at the next worship service. The congregation will be glad to help out with hay offerings."

Rudy held his hands palms out. "Denki, Bishop, but I can afford to use my hay to feed the stock cows. Others may need the aid more than I do if the fires keep happening."

Bishop Bontrager nodded. "Did you know that John Lapp's barn was set on fire?"

"Nah, John, Nurse Hal and her parents were over at our house Thursday. He did not say anything," Rudy declared.

"That is the night it happened," Elton said.

"Do much damage?" Levi Yoder asked.

"Nah, the Lapps found the fire in time to put it out with the help of the fire department. The arsonist hit Nurse Hal over the head and intended to let her burn with the barn. She is lucky the dog and animals woke everyone up," Elton told him.

Rudy looked worried. "That is too bad. What was Nurse Hal doing in the barn that time of night?"

"John said something about her checking on a new goat she bought that would not stay in the pen," Elton said.

"Ach, nah!" Rudy looked contritely at his shoes. "Was she hurt?"

"Bad enough, Brother Rudy. She had to go to the hospital over night. I'm surprised she is here today. She has been on bed rest because of a concussion until yesterday. She helped with the lunch yesterday for the school children and tended Mark Yoder. The boy stepped on a nail that went all the way through his shoe and foot. That was quite a day for her, and here she is back again today," Elton said.

"Gute thing Nurse Hal is tough, I reckon," Levi Yoder praised.

"Part of Bender Road Timber burnt," Amos Coblentz added.

"Nah, the timber!" Elton exclaimed. "When did that happen?"

"Friday night. A rumspringa party was taking place in the timber. I hear the teenagers got out just in time," Amos said.

"Where is all this going to end?" Rudy implored.

"We must pray the person setting the fires sees the light soon," Bishop Bontrager said.

All the men removed their straw hats as Jonah Stolfus said, "We will have a prayer yet."

As soon as the bishop ended the prayer, the women served plates of beef stew, pickled cabbage and applesauce. The thick slabs of homemade bread, everyone had smelled that morning, was passed.

With her shy smile, Ella Miller served the lemonade she made. She had to return to the coolers several times to refill her pitcher.

Jason, the crane operator, stopped eating to say, "This is the best apple butter I've ever tasted. In fact, I can't remember when I've enjoyed such a delicious meal. I guess this is why Amish women are known for their cooking."

The women, within earshot, reddened at the compliment. They weren't used to anyone complimenting them. Jonah Stolfus caught the modest way his wife looked at him and answered for the women. "Our humble denki for your kind words, Jason. The women find joy in sharing the bounty we have. It is a part of who we are, and that is all."

Bishop Bontrager added, "Jason, we believe as the verse says in Ecclesiastes. Do not righteous over much."

The women, girls and smaller children ate after the last of the men and boys went back to work. Hal sat down with her plate beside Redbird and Beth so she could help the girls when they needed it. Not that she'd admit it out loud, but it felt good to get off her feet.

She noticed Wanda in a conversation with Stella Strutt at the end of the next table. They looked her direction a second. Stella went back to waving her hands around as she talk. Hal had an uneasy feeling she was right about Stella causing trouble between the newest members and her.

Women around Hal talked about setting dates for quilting bees. Those gatherings always brought women together to do the painstaking work of stitching a quilt while offering a venue to visit and share news.

Others discussed an applesauce frolic to cook the later apple crop and can applesauce for winter.

Hal heard Stella Strutt's loud voice say, "I will have a quilting bee a week from today. A week from today that is. For those in my neighborhood that are interested. Interested indeed. It will be a gute way for Sister Wanda Bruner here by me to get acquainted with us. Acquainted with us she needs to be."

As Stella's neighbor women agreed, Wanda said, "I would be glad to come. Quilting frolics are fun."

Rudy Briskey's wife, Martha, said, "Perhaps, your sister will be well enough to join us so we can meet her."

"Perhaps, but I cannot say for sure," Wanda agreed halfheartedly. "Gladys did not feel well enough to come today."

Martha suggested, "Maybe you should have Nurse Hal check out your sister. She might be able to help."

Wanda glanced at Stella's stern face before she answered. "We will keep that in mind."

Margaret sat down by Hal. "Should you be here today? Levi just told me what happened to you."

"I'm all recht as long as I sit down when I'm tired. I wouldn't want to miss this day for anything in the world," Hal said gleefully.

"You have helped out all morning. I have not seen you sit down once to rest during that time until now," Margaret corrected sternly.

"I'm fine so don't worry," Hal replied.

Jane Bontrager laid her fork down. She patted Hal's arm and spoke to the other women. "Each of the fires seems to be more dangerous than the others. Hal, you were attacked which could have turned out much worse. The party in Bender Timber would have been a real tragedy for our teenagers if they had not been warned in time."

"We must pray this person is caught soon before something really tragic happens," Mary Mast said in her quiet voice. "Do take care of yourself, Nurse Hal. We need you to be well."

"We've practically had to sit on her to keep her down for a few days like the doctor ordered," Aunt Tootie complained.

"For awhile we thought we might have to fetch Emma to help us keep Hal in bed," Nora said, winking at Emma.

"I would have made sure she minded, but I think you two did well enough. Hallie seems to be feeling better," Emma said, studying her step mother. "You really should rest this afternoon though, Hallie. If you feel the need to go home, just let me

104

know. I will take you. This might be too long a day for you."

"Denki, dear. I'll keep that in mind," Hal told her.

As Emma ate, she studied the teenage boys that had sit across the road in the field all morning. They watched the barn go up as though it was just a show for their amusement. They crossed the road long enough to eat with the men but didn't stay to work. Now they had taken their places in the field again and lit their cigarettes. If they had thought they could get away with it, they would be sipping cans of beer. That would have gotten they sent home, and they knew it.

They were the next rumspringa generation, and a hard looking bunch they were. She was so glad Noah and Daniel hadn't wanted to join that group. She was proud they were among the men working hard to put up the barn.

Albert Jostle, the oldest boy from the Hosteler compound lined up on the ground with his brothers, Sam and Will. It didn't seem to bother them their father, Jake, was working on the barn and their mother, Ada, helped with the luncheon.

Joining them were some of Emma's former pupils, Mark Bender, Rueban Rogies and Matthew Stoll. She hoped Mark and Rueban would come to their senses eventually and join the church. They were good boys.

Matthew worried her the most. He had always been a trouble maker. Emma knew he had a soft spot where she was concerned, but he was a dare devil. He found it so easy to go along with the wrong crowd. He reminded her so much of Eli Yutzy. At the sudden thought of Eli, Emma bowed her head. She said a quick prayer that Eli was safe and happier in the English world than he'd been in her world. She knew his family still missed him and set a plate at the table for every meal, hoping for Eli's return home.

Emma tapped her chin with a finger. "I think I should give those lazy boys in the field a piece of mind for not helping."

"Emma, you be careful. You might make the wrong boy mad at you. No telling what he'd do out of spite," Hal warned.

Emma narrowed her eyes at Hal. "Was ist letz?"

"I suppose I should have said something sooner. Bishop

Bontrager asked Noah and Daniel to go to that drinking party in Bender timber. They listened to see if any of the boys bragged about starting the fires," Hal related. "Your brothers told us Albert bragged about not being afraid of the arsonist. He poured a small bottle of orange juice in his vodka so we know he had access to the bottles.

When Noah and Daniel got tired of standing around, they left. No sooner were they out of the clearing when they heard Albert yell the timber was on fire. He came out of the underbrush. The boys thought he might have set the fire for the excitement of watching the other kids scramble to leave."

"Sounds like something he would do," Emma snapped.

Hal squeezed her hand. "You must go easy with this. Remember what a hard time everyone gave the Jostles when they moved here. We don't want to start any rumors to accuse one of their family falsely."

Emma couldn't help herself. "Just the same, me telling them they need to help build the barn would not hurt. Someone should do it." She left the table and marched across the road.

Albert looked her up and down as she came toward them. He elbowed Matthew Stoll next to him to get his attention.

Ellen halted in front of the lazy boys. With her arms crossed over her chest, she tilted her head to one side, giving each of them a hard look.

Albert focused on the front of her blouse, flicked his tongue out over his lips and gave her a wicked grin. "What is your problem, Teacher?"

The way that boy looked at her made Emma's skin crawl.

"Teacher, you are standing right in our way. We can not see what is happening," Albert's brother, Will, complained.

"You would have a much better view if you lent a hand. Pick up a hammer and help get this barn built," Emma insisted.

"Ach nah, with all those men over there, does it look like to you they need our help?" Matthew Stoll asked. He ducked his head when she narrowed her eyes at him.

"There is more than enough workers. We would just be in the way," Mark Bender agreed.

106

"That is just an excuse, and you know it. Many hands make light work. Everyone of you would be appreciated by the men if you helped out," Emma lectured.

"Besides, we just came to watch the frolic," Rueban Rogies added honestly. "We had no notion to work."

"Praise God that not everyone in this community thinks the way you boys do. Jonah Stolfus would not have a barn to milk his cows in if they did." Emma looked at Albert and thought about what her brothers said about him. "Perhaps, it is because of one or more of you that Jonah lost his barn."

She turned to leave and heard one of the boys grumble, "What is that supposed to mean?"

Emma stalked across the road, wondering why she'd bothered to talk to them. With her head down, she didn't see Bishop Bontrager until she bumped into him. He put his hands out and grabbed her shoulders. "Ach, I am so sorry, Elton. I need to watch where I am going for sure," Emma apologized.

"I reckoned you were deep in troubled thought from that frown I saw on your face. I take it you did not have any luck recruiting the boys in the field to help," Elton said, nodding their direction.

"Nah, they would not budge, but they sure moved fast enough when we hollered it was time to eat," fumed Emma.

"You meant well. Denki for trying. Just leave those young men to me. I will work their laziness into my sermon for the next worship service. Maybe pointing their faults out will shame them," he said wistfully.

The teenage girls washed the dishes, and the women did the table clean up. Hal scraped bits of food off into plastic ice cream buckets and stacked the plates. Wanda came for a stack of dirty plates. Hal smiled at her. "This is a busy day, Sister Wanda, but a great way to get to know all the people in the community and then some, ain't so?"

"Jah," Wanda said curtly. She carried the stack of plates to the dishwashers table.

Hal grimaced as she roughly scraped a plate with a knife. *I just knew Stella got to her.*

Jane placed more dirty plates on the end of the table to be scraped. "Easy on the plate, Sister Hal. What has ruffled your feathers?"

Hal twisted to look around them and explained softly, "Wanda Bruner has been cool toward me ever since she talked to Stella Strutt. I'm just sure she is unfriendly because of something Stella Strutt said."

"Don't worry." Jane chuckled. "It seems like I am always saying not to worry to you lately. You're becoming worse than a setting hen clucking over her chicks. I will visit with Wanda and straighten out whatever Stella told her."

Hal sighed. "Denki, that makes me feel better."

Margaret Yoder brought a stack of plates to Hal. She admired the barn framework and took a deep breath. "Smell fresh cut wood in the air. Sure enough, it is gute to see new wood going up for the Stolfus barn."

"Jah, it is," Hal said, taking her own deep breath. She needed the intake of air more to stay on her feet than out of appreciation for the barn rising up.

The frolic ended around six that evening. Chicken Plucker Jonah said he believed enough work had been done for one day. They all needed to go home and rest up to work another day after they finished their own chores.

Families headed home, richer in the knowledge their brethren's barn would soon be completed. Their role as tradition bearers would be fulfilled.

The Stolfus barn was under a tinned roof the next day, workers painted the walls red and others put the finishing touches inside the barn such as stalls. After that, the nine thousand square-foot barn was back in business.

Thirty eight dairy cows, with patchy coats, munched hay on the first floor. Horses would be moved back later that week from the Nisely farm. In the next week, wagon loads of donated hay fill the second story.

In the middle of the night while so many work weary Amish slept like a log from their last, long, hard day, a lone rider rode into the school house yard. The darkness was thick with a foggy mist. The damp coolness helped to cool the rider's body now heated by fever and lent the rider strength to ride. The waves of dense fog gave the rider confidence. No one would see the school until the deed was well over with. At least, the hope was that this act would be more successful than the other fires that were found too soon.

The students were given time off from school to help build the barn for Jonah Stolfus. They needed to be taught a lesson. Plain children should determine wisely not to help certain people that do not deserve it. Certainly not Jonah Stolfus, a woman killer.

Besides, why did Amish children need a school anyway? Children should be taught all they needed to know at home. It is easier on children that are different if they do not have to be picked on by bullies. I want to stop them from being picked on like I was.

The rider brought a juice bottle from one pocket of the jacket and a few matches from the other.

No need for me to get off the horse for this. It will be too hard to mount again out here in the open with this sore leg. I'll pour the kerosene on the door and around the frame just like I did the corn shocks. That should be enough to start the fire.

Once the juice bottle was empty, the rider slung it against the door. The bottle slid down the door and stopped. A struck match thrown in the spill was just enough to explode. Whoosh! The scared horse shied and bucked. In a weakened condition, it took much of the rider's strength to hang on.

Once the horse had taken off for the road, the rider gave him his head. "All recht, go home, Jack."

The horse headed back west down the country road to Bender timber in the ever thickening fog. Travel was easy enough if a body didn't want to get caught. The trees' shifting shadows were made for hiding in the bad visibility. The rider leaned against the draft horse's neck and held on tight. No need to worry. Jack knew his way back to the barn.

109

Chapter 10

Friday morning, school could be in session since the children didn't need to work on the barn. That morning, Emma drove her buggy into the school driveway and halted the horse. At first, she couldn't fathom why she wasn't seeing the school building. All that was in front of her were smoldering ashes and eye stinging smoke wisps.

"Ach nah! Why my school?" Emma yelled to the silence and broke into tears. She climbed from the buggy and walked as close as she dared to the foundation. She had trouble believing her eyes, but there the disaster was.

Not anything left to be save. Her school was gone. In her mind, she saw the room as it had been with the blackboard on the back wall. The library books shelves Adam built on the north wall under the row of window and all the books. Her desk and the rows of pupils' desks were just a memory. At the entry way, the coat pegs, lunch box shelf and wood box now reduced to ashes.

Emma clenched her hands tight together at her side and glared toward Heaven. "Lord, how could anyone be this hateful toward children to destroy their school? I do not understand a person who is so spiteful."

Instantly, the answer to comfort her popped into her head as if it came from the Lord. Emma remembered the verse,

110

"And to him that smites you on the one cheek offer also the other; and him that takes away your coat forbid not to let him take your shirt, also. Emma knelt on ground blackened by ashes scattered by the breeze over the yard, turning the grass gray. "Lord, I'm sorry for my outburst. I spoke out of anger, because I felt such a loss for the children, and jah, I admit it. The loss is mine, too.

Please give me the strength to talk to my pupils when they arrive this morning. I must try to make them see what you have just shown me. We must turn the other cheek and pray for the arsonist to come to his senses, before he harms someone in a fire." Emma took a deep breath. "And forgive the children if they do not quite see, as clearly as I do, your message. They are young. They are the ones who have lost the most, their beloved school. It will be hard for them to remember the saying I drilled into them. JOY means Jesus is first, you are last, and others are in between. We all need to embrace our faith and beliefs this day. Amen."

Emma wiped her eyes when she heard a buggy coming. It carried the first of her pupils. As soon as she sent all of the children home, she drove to the nearest phone shed to call the sheriff. Emma explained what happened and added there would be no need for the fire trucks. The damage was done. The fire had burned itself out except for the smoldering ashes.

"I'll be right out to look around. You want to wait for me, Mrs. Keim?" the sheriff asked.

"Jah, I will wait," Emma said solemnly.

She drove back to the school yard and stayed in the buggy until Sheriff Dawson drove in. The tall, lean man parked his patrol car under a tree and came to meet her. Grimly, he stared at the smoldering pit. "This is quite a loss. I can tell from the look on your face you're suffering. I'm so sorry."

Emma hopped from the buggy. "Denki, I feel bad for the pupils as much as for myself. It hurts them to think someone can be this mean."

"Well, let me look around. I might find some evidence left behind. We found some at the other fires," the sheriff said.

Emma knitted her fingers together in front of her and leaned against her buggy. "I'll stay here out of your way."

Dawson strode over to the foundation and searched in front and around his shiny, polished shoes until he reached where the door had been. He pulled a purple disposable glove and clear evidence sack out of his jacket pocket. After Dawson slid the glove on, he bent over to pick up a sliver of white plastic which he bagged. A few feet from the former entry way, he picked up a small plastic lid and put it in the bag. "Here is what I was looking for. This tells me it was the same fellow that set all the fires."

Emma closed the distance between the sheriff and herself. "What is it you found?"

"A piece of a small orange juice bottle sold in most grocery and convenience stores. That's what the kerosene was in. The fires haven't quite burnt all of the plastic bottles, and the lid is always somewhere close. Hoof tracks of a large farm horse are always where the fires started. The person is Amish or wants us to think he is.

We have a partial print on the lid found in Rudy Briskey's cornfield and DNA from the blood on Jonah Stolfus's barbed wire fence. We just need to catch the guy that matches our evidence."

Emma folded her arms around herself in a hug and stared at the ashes. "I sure hope you do and soon. Plain people's luck may run out. Someone will be killed in one of these awful fires.

Sheriff, I do not like to point fingers, but I have always felt Joe Jostle's boys might have been in trouble before they moved here. Especially, the older one, Albert. He is taking full advantage of rumspringa now which means he drinks, smokes and takes liberties with English girls while he disrespects his elders.

My brothers say they saw Albert Jostle using a small orange juice bottle to mix liquor in at a timber party. Right after that, Albert walked into the timber and came back to tell everyone to run from a fire.

The whole family is standoffish for some reason. The

parents are better than they were, but they still do not try to fit in much. I feel they are standoffish, because they are hiding something in their past."

Sheriff Dawson pushed his hat back off his forehead. "Thanks for bringing this up. I'll check out the family and see if there's anything they're hiding."

Emma wiped a tear from her cheek. "I'm going to stop by my parents now and tell them about this. I do not feel like sitting home alone anyway. Daed is one of the school board directors. He can get a hold of the other two."

When she walked into the kitchen, Hal stopped kneading bread to rush to her. "Emma, I was beating the dough so hard I didn't hear you drive in. This is a school day. What are you doing here?" She sensed the news wasn't good from the look of woe on Emma's face. "What's wrong? Adam all recht?"

"Jah, Adam is gute. Some horrible person burnt the school last night clean to the ground." Emma hated to say the words which made the event so very true.

"Ach nah, the school is gone?" Hal led Emma to the table and pulled a chair out for her.

"Jah, it is. I waited for the children to come and sent them home. Watching the hurt looks on their faces when they saw the smoking pit that used to be their school was the hardest thing I have ever had to do. I called the sheriff. He came out and looked around," Emma said. "Where is Daed? I need him to tell the other directors for me."

"Your father's walking around the hay field, checking the fence. Deer are hard on fences this time of year when they jump from field to field. He should be back by lunch. Did Sheriff Dawson find anything?" Hal asked anxiously.

"Jah, another piece of a small orange juice bottle that held the kerosene and the lid that might have a finger print on it. A horse's tracks coming in the yard, close by the school door where the fire was set and back to the road. Large enough tracks to be a draft work horse."

Hal looked confounded. "There doesn't seem to be any reason behind any of the fires. Why would anyone burn the

113

school?"

"I keep thinking about the boys from the Hosteller compound. Those three boys look like they could be responsible and call their actions pranks," Emma said. "Maybe I should have kept quiet, but I mentioned them to the sheriff. He said he would check on the Jostle boys past before they came here. Especially Albert."

"Noah and Daniel think the same thing, but you can't accuse the boys without proof," Hal warned. "The person who burnt the Stolfus barn cut his leg on the barbed wire fence when he climbed over it. The sheriff has a sample of blood. If he gets a DNA match from that, he will know he has the right person."

Emma put her hands over her face. "The sheriff told me. That is all well and gute, but in the meantime, what are my pupils to do for a school? It will take maybe two weeks to organize and a day or two to build the school. We will be so far behind by that time the children will never catch up."

Hal looked thoughtful. "Don't worry yet." She chuckled. "Funny Jane had to say that twice to me recently. Just so you know, I picked that advice up from her, and I can't swear that it has taken hold of me yet. What you need is a make shift school until you can move back into a new building."

"Have you any suggestions?"

"Jah, has Adam filled the upstairs above the store with furniture?"

Emma's face lit up. "Nah, he does some varnishing there sometimes is all."

"There's your answer. Ask that generous husband of yours for the use of the shop's upstairs until the new school is built. You will need tables and seats. We can get the bench wagon sent to Adam's furniture shop. Wa-la, a makeshift school," Hal said, wiping a tear off Emma's cheek with her finger.

Emma felt as if a great mountain had been lifted off her shoulders. She paused to listen. "It is very quiet around here this morning. Where are Mammi Nora and Aendi Tootie?"

It was Hal's turn to look sad. "Packing. Dad is ready to go

114

home. He says he wants to leave before winter sets in. They are leaving in the morning."

"It has been a long time they have been here They are probably ready for the peace and quiet of their own homes and less excitement than they had here this time," Emma said wisely.

"Would you and Adam like to come over tonight for supper since this is their last night here?" Hal invited.

"Jah, that would be gute. I could use a happy distraction for a change. We will come early enough for me to help you cook," Emma said.

"That's great! I've missed your hand in the kitchen," Hal said, smiling as if Emma had given her a gift.

"What would you like to fix for this last supper?" Emma asked.

"My, that sounds so biblical. Why don't we ask our guests of honor what they would like to eat," suggested Hal. "I'll see if they will stop packing long enough to discuss this with us."

She went to the foot of the stairs, and Emma stood behind her. "Mom, Dad, Aunt Tootie, could you come down here for a minute?"

The three appeared on the landing.

"Why?" Jim asked.

"Oh, Emma is here," cried Nora. "Come on, Tootie. We can take the time to visit with her. Jim, it must be coffee break time."

They tromped down the stairs and followed Hal and Emma to the table.

Jim puzzled, "Wait a minute! Emma, why are you here in the middle of the morning?"

"That's right. This is a school day," Nora said.

"It would have been, but someone burnt the school last night." Emma brushed tears from her cheeks.

"That is just plain too awful," Aunt Tootie asserted, stamping her foot.

"That's the way we feel about it," Hal said. "Now sit down, and I'll pour the coffee."

"What are you going to do for a school, Emma?" Nora asked.

"Hallie had the answer. We will hold school in the top of Adam's store until a new school can be built," Emma told her.

"That is great news. When times are tough, the tough get going," Jim said, giving Emma a hug.

Hal said, "Now before Emma leaves to make plans for setting up the school room, I've invited Adam and her to come for your gute bye supper tonight. We want to know what each of you would most like to eat so Emma and I can fix your favorite dishes."

"Let me think a minute." Aunt Tootie took a sip of coffee.

"I sure like your raw apple cake," Jim said.

"The Pennsylvania Dutch green bean dish you fix is my favorite," Nora said.

"Aunt Tootie?" Hal questioned.

"How about the chicken corn soup we had at one of the worship service luncheons? That was really tasty. I loved your shoo fly pie, but Jim is right. The raw apple cake is good, too," Tootie said wistfully.

"We can have the soup, both desserts and homemade ice cream," Emma told her. "Plus, fried potatoes and tomato gravy."

Hal planned, "For meat, I'll open some canned pork roast."

Jim said, "We're leaving John out. What do you think he'd like to have for this supper?"

"I know," Hal said. "He will want a big pan of Emma's light, fluffy biscuits."

Nora laughed. "Slow down. You cook too much, and there won't be any room for our plates on the table."

"Now, Mom, don't discourage us. Emma's left overs are gute especially when my two cooks take off for home and leave me in the kitchen alone," Hal teased.

Emma stood up. "I should leave now if I'm going to ready a substitute school for Monday. I will find Daed and talk to him before I take off. See you three tonight," She hugged her mammi, dawdi and aendi before she left.

Nora and Aunt Tootie fixed a light lunch of creamed corn, sausage cakes and vanilla pudding. After they ate, Hal hunted up the ingredients for the evening meal while Nora and Aunt Tootie did the dishes. She liked to be prepared so they didn't have to rush later on. Besides if she stayed busy, she didn't have time to feel sad about the loss of the school or think about how much she'd miss her parents and Aunt Tootie.

Mid afternoon, the women sat down at the table for a coffee break. They reminisced about the summer and fall and how quickly their vacation had passed.

"It'll seem lonesome for all of us when you're gone," Hal said. "We count the days until your next visit. You will be able to come back next summer, won't you, Mom?"

"We should be able to if our health holds up. I know Jim will be eager to come, and I sure enjoyed being here," Nora said.

Nora and Hal looked at Aunt Tootie who was quietly staring into her coffee cup to avoid the conversation.

"How about you, Aunt Tootie?" Hal asked.

Aunt Tootie looked pensive. "I hate to say this, but I'm not sure. Let's wait and see how I feel in the spring. I don't know if I can take another summer like this one. What with someone trying to burn your barn and hurt you, your mean rooster attacking me, that goat trying to eat my clothes right off of me and a skunk sleeping next door to me. I think it will take a good long time for me to get over this stay."

"I'm so sorry, Aunt Tootie. I hope you recover by the time Mom and Dad are ready to return," Hal consoled. "Listen, I hear a buggy coming in. Emma and Adam must be here."

As they waited for the company to come inside, they heard them walk up the steps and Emma say, "Turn loose of my apron. Get away from us, Goat. Go back to the barn."

Aunt Tootie grumbled softly to Nora, "See this is what I was trying to tell you. The animals around here are too friendly."

"Oh, nah! Gano is taking over where Tom Turkey left off.

She has become the official Lapp company greeter," Hal said as she left to help Emma and Adam in the house.

All the talking woke up Redbird and Beth from their nap. As soon as they saw Adam standing in the living room, they popped up from the quilt and ran to grab him around the leg. Both little girls squeezed Adam so tightly, he couldn't move.

Redbird smiled up at him. "My Adam."

"My Adam," Beth said argumentatively.

Redbird shoved at her.

Adam's face turned stern as he put one forefinger over the other and rubbed it at both of them. The girls lowered their eyes and pouted.

Adam picked them both up and smiled at them. That earned him a hug from each.

Emma watched, thinking what a good father Adam would make, but she teased, "I sure see how I rate around here when Adam is with me."

Aunt Tootie rushed to her and hugged her. "Don't worry, dear. The rest of us are happy to see you."

Emma laughed. "Now I feel better."

The women took on the task of fixing a large supper that Jim, Nora and Aunt Tootie would remember. Hal and Emma found it hard to stay cheerful, but they managed. Hal's mind wandered to how lonesome she'd be after tomorrow morning when her family left for home. Emma got a heart sinking feeling every time she thought about how much she'd miss her school house until the new one was built.

Supper went well. At devotion, John read the bible, concentrating on Matthew in chapter five and verse forty four. Emma had the feeling her father aimed the reading at her.

"But I say unto you, Love your enemies, bless them that curse you, do good to them that hate you, and pray for them which despitefully use you, and persecute you," John read. "Let us pray now." Everyone bowed their heads as John prayed for the soul of the arsonist and his awakening to the destruction he'd done before others were harmed. John added the Plain children needed guidance and understanding while they tried to deal with this latest act of evil.

By the time devotions were over, Redbird and Beth's heads were nodding. Hal said it was time the two sleepy heads were in bed, and Emma offered to help her put them there.

While they undressed the girls, Hal said, "I think tonight went pretty well, ain't so?"

"Jah. I've tried very hard not to think about how sad I feel about the school," Emma said.

"I know what you mean. I'd very easily break into tears before my parents and Aunt Tootie have even taken off if I gave their going much thought." Hal gave a mournful sigh as she put the nightgown over Beth's head.

Emma slipped Redbird's arms into her nightgown and laid her on the pillow. She kissed the girls on the cheek. "Go to sleep, little redbird and sweet Beth." Emma's soft voice was all it took for the girls to close their eyes and doze off. Emma turned to Hal and folded her arms over her chest. "Maybe what you need is some happy news to concentrate on."

"Was ist los?"

"What is up is how would you like to know you are going to be a mammi?"

Hal digested that out of the blue admission and squealed. "You're serious?"

"Jah, one of the reasons the school house burning bothers me is this will be my last year of teaching. I will always remember the arsonist's awful act as part of my last year." Emma bit her lower lip to keep from crying.

"Oh, but keep thinking about what you have to look forward to now. I'll bet Adam is excited about your news," Hal said.

"Ach, jah!" Emma gave Hal a wide smile.

Hal hugged her. "I am so happy for you. Fudge! I'm even happier for John and me. Wait until he hears we are going to be grandparents. Are you going to tell him or can I?"

"You can if you want to," offered Emma hesitantly.

"I might have to, or I'll burst waiting for you to find a quiet moment to talk to him," Hal said.

"All recht, you tell Daed."

"Well, since we're confessing, I haven't told anyone not even John yet, but you're going to be a big sister again." The words rushed from Hal's mouth, and she waited for a reaction from Emma.

"Our children will grow up together. I think that is a voonderball gute thing. Turn about is only fair. Do I get to tell Adam your news?"

"Jah, that would be gute," Hal said.

Emma put her hand to her cheeks, and her eyes sparkled. "I just thought of something. You can be the midwife to deliver you grandchild into the world."

Hal slowly shook her head. "Emma, I'm not sure I want that responsibility. Maybe we better ask Rachel Kitzmiller to help with you."

"Nah, it has to be you. It would be my luck Rachel would go to town the day I need her. If you recall, that is what she did to you," Emma said stubbornly.

"All recht, young lady, but turn about is only fair. If I help you, you have to be my midwife," Hal shot back.

Emma frowned a second before she broke into a smile. "All recht. I will do it."

Chapter 11

The next morning was a lonely start to the day after Hal's parents and aunt left for home. Redbird and Beth wandered from room to room, calling for their grandparents and aunt. Hal tried to explain Dawdi, Mammi and Aendi went to their home far away, but the little girls weren't buying it.

Hal was ready for a diversion by the time Margaret Yoder, Roseanna Nisely and Martha Briskey all drove in at the same time. They came to help cook molasses at Sugar Camp.

Hal met them on the porch.

"You ready to go while it is still cool. I believe the day will warm up from the way it feels," Margaret said.

"All I have left to load is our lunch basket, a quilt and the water cooler in the buggy and the girls, of course," Hal said.

Margaret opened the screen door and scooped up Redbird. "We can help carry. I caught me a girl." She tickled Redbird's belly as she carried the giggling girl to Hal's buggy.

"Jah, it will be a gute, warm, fall day," Martha agreed, taking a deep breath of fresh air as she placed Beth beside Redbird. "The vat will make us hot enough without added heat from the sun."

Roseanna followed Hal to the kitchen and picked up the dish towel covered wicker basket full of sandwiches, bags of chips and a covered cake pan.

Hal chattered as they headed for the buggy. "I'm not only ready I'm excited. I didn't get involved when Emma was in charge. I know this is something that has passed down from generation to generation in the Plain community. I want to learn all about molasses making so I can do it from now on. When they are a little older, I'll pass on how to make molasses to my little girls." She tossed two quilts in the buggy to sit on at Sugar Camp and placed a two gallon cooler of water in next. "I've been waiting all summer for the cane to get ready to harvest."

Hal drove down the lane and across the hay field. They passed the cane field which was now rows of stubbles and green piles of cane. The day before, Noah and Daniel stripped the canes of their leaves by cutting swiftly along each side of the stalks. Next the boys removed the head of seeds and cut the five to eleven foot stalks off close to the ground.

As the women drove by, Noah and Daniel placed arm loads of cane on a hay wagon to bring to Sugar Camp. Hal stuck her hand out the open window and waved. "I'd never seen sorghum cane growing before I saw this field. I think it looks much like corn without the ears."

"Sure enough," Margaret agreed. "Except instead of tassels on top, cane has a seedy head cluster."

"When the canes mature in four months, it is time to harvest. That is just the start of the hard work through the whole process to make sorghum molasses," Martha said.

"Molasses sure will be gute this winter," Roseanna said.

"Sure enough," Hal agreed. "I used the last of my supply to make two shoo fly pies for supper last night."

"That was dessert for your family?" Margaret asked.

"Jah, I gave my parents and Aunt Tootie their choice of food for supper since it was their last night with us. Shoo fly pie was Aunt Tootie's pick for dessert. Dad wanted a raw apple cake. Emma came over to help me so she mixed up the cake. We had most of the cake left over last night so it is our lucky day. We'll eat the raw apple cake for dessert today."

Martha shook her head sadly. "Emma must be beside

herself about the school house burning."

"I know she is," Margaret agreed.

Roseanna Nicely nodded. "So are my children. They cannot understand how someone could burn their school."

"Jah, Emma was very upset that someone was that cruel to her students," Hal said.

The cane field wasn't far from the small pie shaped pasture on the back side of John's farm known as Sugar Camp. The sorghum mill had been built a century ago. It was a long framed building open on one side. Noah and Daniel had done a good job of cutting a large supply of wood. They piled it by the building to fuel the fire under the pans.

Hal parked the buggy in the shade of the grove of burr oak trees. "My, this is a pretty time of year with the timbers so full of color."

Roseanna sighed. "Jah, and watch the leaves fall like feathers flying in the wind from hens. Will not be long until the trees will be bare. I never look forward to the signs of winter."

The women climbed out of the buggy. Margaret spread one of the blankets on the ground. Hal placed Redbird on the blanket, and Martha put Beth beside her. Redbird yawned while Beth rubbed her eyes.

"Lay down, girls. Take a nap," Hal said.

"You think they will nap this time of morning?" Martha asked.

Hal covered the girls up with the other blanket and walked toward the mill. "Usually they wouldn't, but they ran from room to room all morning, looking for their grandparents and aunt. For once, the girls are tired and ready for a nap which is gute for me. I won't have to watch them while we get started."

Along the south of the building was the fireplace chimney. Attached to the chimney was a brick oven, with an enormous pan covering the top. Its size was eight feet long and four feet wide. The pan had four compartments with gates that opened from one compartment to the next. The pan ran downhill just enough to keep the cane juice flowing through the pans.

Outside the mill was the machine which crushed the cane

stalks. Sweet green juice ran into a trough which led to the first pan in the vat.

The machine shredded the stalks by the horse walking around and around in a circle. His hooves had already tramped the grass into the dirt. By the end of the day, the horse's hooves would wear the path down to a deep groove.

Noah drove the wagon, loaded with cane, close to the crushing machine. He called to Hal, "We have enough juice in the first pan for you to start cooking."

"Denki, we're ready to go," Hal replied. "Wait until we empty the pan before you start crushing again."

Martha picked up the hoe like tool, leaning in the corner, to stir the juice. Roseanna went to the creek after a bucket of water to wash the tools. Margaret and Hal lifted the mesh off the pan and carried it over to the timber edge to dump off the cane pieces.

Margaret opened the gate on the pan. She stirred around the pan as the last of the green liquid swirled into the next pan. She shut the gate, helped Hal replace the screen and waved at the boys. "Now start the next batch."

Hal picked up an arm load of wood to put under the compartment with the juice in it. Margaret splashed kerosene on the wood and lit the pile. Soon the pan had flames licking up out of the bricks and along the sides of the pan.

Smoke billowed around the women as they stirred, stinging their eyes. Sweat beaded up on their foreheads and dripped down their faces. Margaret wiped her face with her apron tail. "Denki to the woman that invented the apron."

"How do you know it was a woman that invented aprons?" Hal asked.

Margaret surmised, "It had to be. Men do not worry about covering their clothes to keep clean, and they have a handkerchief to wipe their face."

Noah helped Daniel feed the cane slowly on one side of the crusher. The rollers in the mill crushed the stalks and shredded the canes dry of the juice which ran out of the cane into the first pan in the mill.

The vat was divided into four pans so several batches could be cooked at one time, facilitating a continuous cooking process. So for the next eight to twelve hours, the juice cooked at a slow boil. The women stirred with long-handled tools shaped like a hoe and called a skimmer.

By the time, the boys had enough cane shredded for another batch to fill the catch pan, the first batch had thickened a little and changed to a greenish amber. Margaret lifted the gate and moved the juice into the third pan. That batch was cooked until it lost all the green color. By that time, the syrup was darker and thicker. Margaret opened the gate to let the syrup into the fourth pan. The sorghum cooked until it was mahogany color and quite thick. The first batch took eight hours, and each batch was an hour behind that one.

Martha ran a skimmer over the top of the syrup in the pans and remove the impurities. Hal watched her lift the scum out with her hoe into a pail. "Why are you doing that?

"The whole time the juice is cooking, until the last pan or two, it must be skimmed. This involves running this skimmer across the top of the cooking juice to remove the skim that forms which is the impurities cooking out of the juice," Martha said.

"I see. This is such a hot job so when one of you are ready to get away and cool off let me spell you," Hal said. "In the mean time, I'm going after more wood."

When the first batch of juice reached the last pan, Margaret said, "Hal, the sorghum must be watched carefully so it is removed at just the right time. This is the part that takes practice and know-how. Remove it too soon and it will not be done. Wait to long and it will be too thick and have a strong, bitter taste."

"Until I get the hang of this, you better be the one to watch the last pan. I'd hate to ruin the molasses now we have our taste buds set for it," Hal told Margaret. "Why don't you go take a break? Eat lunch and cool off before you take over. I think I can watch the molasses boil down long enough for you to take a break without ruining the batch before you come back."

Margaret laughed. "That sounds like a gute idea to me. You will do fine. Martha, you want to come with me. Roseanna can skim until we get back."

Martha wiped her flushed face on her apron. "Jah, I could use a time to sit and cool down."

"Redbird and Beth are hungry and thirsty by now. You can give them each half a sandwich if they want it," Hal said.

When Margaret and Martha came back, Margaret chuckled. "The girls are rutsching around. You might be glad to have them take another nap."

Hal rolled her eyes. "If only we were so lucky."

"I have them piling the leaves that fell on the quilt by colors. They seemed to like that, but little ones that age do not stick with anything for very long," Martha said sagely.

Hal brought two more glasses from the buggy and filled them from the cooler. She handed one glass to Roseanna and reached under the dish towel to get a sandwich out of the pan. Redbird and Beth watched her take a bite from her sandwich. "You two still hungry? You want to split a sandwich."

The girls nodded no, but they held out their glasses. While they sipped water, the girls put leaves scattered on the quilt in the piles Martha started for them.

"What are you girls doing?" Roseanna asked.

Beth pointed to her pile, picked up another leaf and put on her stack. She looked at Roseanna for approval.

"Very gute, Beth. Such a neat pile."

"What are you doing, Redbird?" Hal asked.

Redbird stared at a red oak leaf in her hand. She raised her pensive face so she could see passed her bonnet bill with a sad face. "Leave?"

"Nah, it is a leaf," Hal said slowly.

Redbird nodded no. "Mammi and dawdi leave?"

"Jah, they went home. We will miss them, ain't so?" Hal said.

Both girls puckered up. Hal held out her arms and let them sit in her lap while she hugged them. After a few minutes, Hal

126

pointed to the birds overhead. The girls chattered about the birds flying from tree to tree, and all the pretty leaf piles they had made.

Finally, Hal said, "How about taking a nap? We will go home soon after you wake up?"

The sound of wagon wheels made the girls straighten up and watch. They pointed at Noah and Daniel coming back.

"Your brothers need to eat. I expect they're hungry." When Noah stopped the wagon by the crushing machine, Hal said, "You two come eat and get a cold drink of water. It is hot work you've done. You can shred that load after you rest."

Hal and Roseanna rose from the blanket and let the boys sit down. "As long as you're here, the girls won't go to sleep. Will you lay them down and cover them up for a nap when you're done eating?"

"Sure enough," Noah said.

As the women walked away, Hal heard Daniel say, "What have you girls been doing?"

"Leaf," Beth's shy voice said.

"Leave us," complained Redbird.

"Nah, Redbird, that is a leaf," Noah corrected.

"Nah, Mammi and Dawdi leave," Redbird said grumpily.

"Jah, they did. We miss them," Noah said. He stuck his hand in the dish pan and pulled out two sandwiches. "Have a sandwich, Daniel."

That afternoon while the women cooked Luke Yoder, Samuel Nisely and Rudy Briskey's sorghum canes, Hal listened to the other women reminisce about past experiences at the sorghum mills.

Margaret stirred the darkening molasses with a paddle as she talked. "I remember helping my mother in Pennsylvania when I was young. The smell of this wood smoke all around us takes me back to those times. Mama would give me a cane stick to dip into the rich, sweet sorghum as it cooked. After warning me not to burn my mouth of course. I have seldom tasted such delicious sorghum as that first time."

Hal leaned down and added sticks to the fire. "We need to

treat the boys and the little girls with a sweet treat like that. It will bring back memories to them some day of this time we spent together at Sugar Camp."

Martha gazed into her compartment as she pushed and pulled on her skimmer. "My dawdi used to hand out little pieces of canes and let us children dip them into the hot molasses, too. Poor dawdi used to love working in his sorghum mill. He died doing what he loved."

"How did that happen?" Roseanna asked, dumping the skim on her hoe in a pail.

"Dawdi fainted after stirring the pans all day. He died of heat stroke a few days later, brought on by working in the sorghum mill."

"How sad. I am so sorry that happened," Roseanna said. "I remember my mama used to make biscuits for us to break into pieces and dunk in a bowl of molasses."

Martha dumped the skim off her shovel. "I remember we used each run we called the pans for some different recipe. First run for lite syrup to put on pancakes. Next run was thicker for using in shoo fly pie. Last run Black Strap molasses was in cookies and gingerbread."

When the last of the sorghum was entirely cooked in the last pan, Margaret raised the little gate at the end of all the pan. Hal went out to the pile of shredded cane and hunted up several ends. She dipped the pieces of cane in the molasses and blew on two of them until they cooled.

Hal carried the dripping cane strips to the quilt. The girls were still napping. She put the cane treats in their drinking glasses for later. She handed Daniel and Noah the remaining two.

By the time she came back to the mill, the syrup had filled a barrel, and it was replace by another. And so on until the entire pan was empty.

Noah and Daniel watched the last batch run into a barrel. That was a very enticing spot for kids of any age. Daniel reached down with a couple of fingers and swiped along the top edge of the barrel. His fingers darkened with licking good syrup. Since Daniel got away with sticking his fingers in the sorghum drips, Noah did the same thing.

Hal spotted the boys with their fingers in their mouths and grinned. "At your age, you boys should have something better to do than suck your fingers."

"Ach, Mama Hal," Daniel said, his face flushing with embarrassment.

When the day was over, the barrels were hauled away. The women cleaned out the brick fireplace. They polished and oiled the pans then placed them up side down on top of the fireplace for the winter.

Noah and Daniel carried out all the hot ashes and coals from the brick foundation under the pan. They scattered the coals in the grove.

With everyone busy during the clean up, no one noticed the barefoot little girls wander toward the grove. They wanted to go into the trees to get a closer look at the pretty birds.

Daniel carried the last bucket of coals out of the sorghum mill. He looked toward the grove and saw the girls disappear in the trees. He took off in a run. "Come back, Redbird! Beth, come back here! Mama Hal, come quick."

"Was ist letz?" Hal asked as she ran after Daniel.

"The girls are in the grove with the live coals," Daniel yelled over his shoulder.

Before they reached the grove, Redbird screamed in pain. By the time Hal and Daniel got to her and Beth, Beth was backing up as Redbird hopped on one foot and cried, "It hurt! It hurt!"

Hal grabbed Redbird and carried her out into the sunlight while Daniel rescued Beth.

By that time, the other women and Noah came to meet them. Hal explained what had happened to Redbird and lifted her right foot to look at the bottom of it. Red welts and water blisters had formed already.

"We need a pan of cool water to place her foot in to take away some of the heat," Hal said. "Can someone get that for me? Redbird isn't going to let go of my neck long enough to put her down."

Margaret grabbed a pan and raced to the creek for the water. The other women packed the lunch supplies in the buggy. Noah and Daniel mounted the horse and trotted for home.

After Redbird had soaked her foot a few minutes, she was calmer. Hal inspected the burn area.

"Is it bad?" Roseanna asked.

"She'll have a scar sure enough," Hal said. Margaret, will you drive home while I hold on to Redbird? I want to keep her foot in the water a little longer."

Chapter 12

After supper, Noah and Daniel went coon hunting for real this time. The boys took Biscuit hunting to get the dog used to trailing for them, before they went out with friends to hunt. The little girls were upstairs in bed. Hopefully, Redbird wouldn't be in too much pain to keep her from sleeping through the night.

Hal decided to work on the mending to keep her mind off the fact she missed her parents and aunt. She sat down on the couch and pulled a pair of Daniel's trousers out of the mending basket. She put a patch over a split knee.

John rocked as he read the Wickenburg Daily newspaper. He folded the newspaper and laid it on his legs.

Hal looked up as the paper rattled. "Any noteworthy news in the Wickenburg Daily."

"An article on the fires around here. Phil King has been working hard to earn his wages for the newspaper again. He interviewed farmers and even went to Yoder Store to catch customers for their opinion of the fires. I am surprised he has not used this for an excuse to come here to get your ideas," John said dryly.

Hal snorted. "Phil knows better than to bother me."

"Sure enough. Maybe he is afraid of you and your skillet," John said, grinning.

Hal folded Daniel's trousers and laid them on the couch.

She reached in the basket for a shirt of Noah's that needed a button. "If fear is what keeps him from pestering me, I will go with that. Mind reading me the article he wrote? I'd like to hear what he said."

"Jah, I can." John unfolded the newspaper. "The story made front page news with a picture of the schoolhouse foundation. It says, The Amish, devout pacifists, were profoundly shaken by the violence that took place in their community recently. But there are no doubt going to be further shocks to come with a torching madman on the loose. Crime is so rare here that members of the Christian sect consider the fires a test of faith. All the while, the Amish have simply turned the other cheek to the arson destruction aimed at them.

"The Amish around here are a quiet, withdrawn community of hard workers. This inferno of destruction has caused them a great deal of income loss and worry for the safety of their families and neighbors," says Malcolm Yoder, owner of Yoder Country Store, in the country south of Wickenburg. He's one of the few outspoken members of the community that didn't mind talking to this reporter.

"With word spreading on radio and television, now the outside world is stopping in at my store, asking questions about the burnings," Malcolm Yoder told me. "They ask directions to see the barn that burnt. I pointed out that we had already set things right for Jonah Stolfus by having a barn raising. Now Jonah Stolfus tells me a steady stream of cars drive by his farm to see the new barn that just went up."

One customer at Yoder Country Store, who asked to leave his name out of the article for fear he might be burned out for speaking up, listened to Malcolm Yoder's comments. This reporter took the opportunity to ask for his thoughts on the arsons. He stated, "The questions brought up among us are about why this is happening to us, and what building will go up in flames next. These evil acts are not limited to our Plain community. English might find their buildings in flames, too."

Some of the Amish are having their faith tested as they keep a watchful eye on their property. One day this reporter traveled to the Amish community south and west of Wickenburg to view the damage for himself. As I passed by a blackened cornfield, I realized what a loss of winter feed this was for Rudy Briskey, the owner. I stopped to ask him to give his thoughts on this matter.

"Why did the arsonist pick on us?" Asked Rudy Briskey. "We believe because we are God's sheep, we mean this person no harm. Matter of fact, we choose to forgive him. If that person was caught after burning a farmer's buildings on a non-Amish place, you might be writing his obituary. That is the difference between English and Plain people."

That made this reporter wonder just how an English farmer would feel about Rudy Briskey's comment. I stopped at the century old Carter family farm to visit with Bud Carter. Here is what he had to say. "I have nothing but respect for the Amish community. We should all be peaceful, more forgiving of others and mind our own business which is their life long practice.

As for how an arsonist who is that mentally sick going to be treated in our justice system, I believe we have good law enforcement officers that will eventually catch the guy. They will see that due process of law is done, and the person will be in prison or a mental institution for a long time.

I can understand how any farmer feels upset that lost his winter feed supply, a barn that houses a large herd of milk cows or the children's school house to such terrible acts.

Rudy Briskey is right. A devastating fire could happen on my farm before this person is caught or at any other non-Amish farm. We should all be vigilant until this sick person is arrested. Am I going to sit up nights to keep watch over my property? Probably not, but my dog is running loose. He is a good watch dog, and my rifle will be close if I need to use it."

After extensive interviews and investigations for this story, this reporter found there could have been even more serious repercussions if it wasn't for our fine Wickenburg Fire Department. The first fire was at Jonah Stolfus's farm with the burning down his dairy barn. The intense heat curled the house siding, coming close to setting the house on fire if the Wickenburg Volunteer fire department hadn't been on scene so fast. Our hats are off to them!

Mr. Stolfus lost some of his livestock to the fire and has others so badly burned they have been sick ever since. His dairy herd's milk production is down because of the fire which means he's losing income. Even with this much loss, Mr. Stolfus considers his family fortunate. If the animals hadn't woke them up, the house would have caught fire, and some of his family might have perished.

Next came the fire to corn shocks in a farm field which was a loss of Rudy Briskey's winter cattle feed. A fire went through that dry field as if the shocks were made out of paper, coming very close to the house before the firemen arrived. If Mr. Briskey's animals hadn't woke him up, the fire trucks might not have made it in time before his house caught fire. As it was, the whole cornfield burnt almost to the house yard.

This reporter understands the next fire was in the barn of John Lapp. In the middle of the night while the family slept, a bale of hay in the barn was set on fire. Mr. Lapp's wife, Nurse Hal, happened to be in the barn to check on a recently purchased milk goat. She was brutally attacked from behind. The hard blow to her head and inhaled smoke was enough to keep her in the hospital overnight. If not for the dog barking, and the upset cows and horses, the barn would have been a total loss with the Amish's well liked Nurse Hallie Lapp unconscious on the barn floor as it burned.

The last fire, a low blow indeed, was the burning of the Amish's innocent children's building of learning, their school house. Of all the senseless acts, this one was the lowest blow.

Now the outside world is coming around, asking questions about the burnings. The fires have left people in this county sympathetic with the Amish Community and nervous about where the arsonist might strike next. This sort of crime is so rare here that members of the Christian sect consider it a test of their faith as much as the Amish do. We all pray the person is caught soon." John folded up the newspaper again.

134

Hal cut the thread from the secured button on the shirt and put away her needle and scissors. "Phil did a gute job of stirring up people to be on guard for another fire. Hopefully if that happens, someone gets a look at the person so he can be arrested the next time. What kind of man is Bud Carter?"

"A gute man. I have known him for years. He would not hurt anyone. He is just trying to send a warning message to the arsonist for all of us like Rudy Briskey did." John smiled. "Last time I talked to Bud was the carriage sale at the salebarn when your father bought the courting buggy. Back then, Bud was trying to impress a woman so that day he bought a Cinderella coach."

Hal giggled. "Where on earth did that come from?"

John shrugged. "I have no idea."

"Did the coach work?" Hal asked.

"Jah, all Bud needed was a matched pair of horses to make it go," John said.

"Nah, John. I meant did he get the woman's attention?"

"Ach, that! Jah, they got married," John said.

"Wait a second. Is Mr. Carter the sister of Susie that owns the Maid Rite? I remember she mentioned she was excited about her brother Bud and his wife expecting a baby when we dined there. That was when we shopped for Emma's wedding dress material," Hal said.

John stifled a yawn. "Jah, that is the family."

Hal looked puzzled. "Millie, the previous owner of the Maid Rite before Susie, was an Alperson. That's Susie's mother. Where does Bud Carter fit in?"

"His mother was married to a Carter that owned the farm Bud farms. She had Bud and Susie. Her husband died and she married an Alperson," John explained.

"I see. This has been a long day. Do we have to wait up for the boys? I'm bushed."

"Me, too," John said, placing the newspaper on the floor by his rocker. "The boys are big enough to take care of themselves. We can go to bed."

As soon as Hal blew out the lamp, she heard John snore.

135

She just remembered Emma's news and had to tell right away. "John, I forgot to tell you something."

"What is it?" John mumbled.

"Emma wants me to share that you're going to be a dawdi next spring," Hal said softly.

John rolled over and stared at Hal. "Why is it you have to save everything you want to surprise me with until I am almost asleep?"

"Sorry, I forgot until now," Hal said.

"You are forgiven with es voonderball gute thing like this," John said as he rolled back on his side.

Hal put her hand on his shoulder. "Wait! Don't go to sleep yet. Not before I tell you that you're going to be a daed next spring, too."

John plopped back over. "Are you sure? I am going to be a daed and a dawdi at the same time?"

"Jah." Hal paused. "Well, nah, maybe not at the same time. We cannot know that, but Emma and I've talked. We're sure we are both expecting. At this moment, she's telling Adam the news, too."

"Adam will make a gute father," John said while he yawned.

"That is what I told Emma. Adam will be so proud, and I am going to be a mammi. How about that?"

Hal waited for John to answer. His reply was a series of long and loud snores.

The Sunday worship service was at Eli and Mary Mast's house. Following the hymn and a prayer by Bishop Bontrager, Deacon Enos Yutzy gave a scripture reading. Next Luke Yoder came forward to give a message. He linked his fingers together in front of him and looked at the congregation. "It is the law of the Ordnung to live a simple life. Are there those among us in our group, maybe some of the youth that are covetous of English conveniences which is against our Ordnung? If we were to introduce modern conveniences into our lives we might start small with a cell phone, television or a transistor radio. I

136

have heard over the years about our youth being attracted to these English items. Maybe a cell phone seems like a small thing, but we have our phone sheds when there is a need to use a phone. Television and radio are a sewer line to the American cesspool. We should avoid them.

As for automobiles and electricity, if we had these things would we not then become dependent on them? Might we begin seeking to prosper beyond our needs to be able to afford to pay for such conveniences? Might that make us put money first in our lives ahead of God and family?

Our buggies take us where we need to go. We do not need shiny new cars that are gas hogs which pollute our environment. Our fields and gardens produce food for our livestock and us. We do not need to spend a huge amount for food with rising prices in the grocery stores. If we only take the time to think about it, we have what we need, and that is enough. We should always be content with what we have." Luke looked toward the back rows filled with teenage boys in the rumspringa age group. "To our youth, I say as you mature you should remember this sermon. One day, you will be able to look back and say Luke Yoder was right."

Daniel felt as if Luke meant the message for Noah and him. He wanted the hard bench seat to swallow him up, but that wasn't going to happen. He wiggled on the seat, feeling guilty for even knowing about Noah's radio.

Luke continued. "We are raised with basic convictions and know to live our life with meaning and purpose. We surrender to God by living in a way that pleases God and by obeying religious authority.

Gelassenheit is layered with many meanings. One such is self surrender. Another is self denial which includes modern conveniences that is not of our world such as computers, cell phones, televisions and radios.

Resigning ourselves to God's will, gentleness, a calm and contented spirit and quiet acceptance of whatever comes is the only way to live.

Take a look some time at a wren. It is as if this tiny brown

137

bird knows Romans chapter twelve verse two first hand. And be not conformed to this world: but be ye transformed by the renewing of your mind. That ye may prove what is that is gute, and acceptable, and the perfect will of God.

The wren perches on fence posts and watches the world go on around it. He is happy to live a simple life, build a small nest for two eggs and eat only what is needed to survive and feed the babies.

The tiny bird is content. How do I know? You can tell by the cheerful songs he sings."

As a demonstration, a wren lit outside the window and warbled a bubbly tune for the congregation. That caused Plain heads to nod, and the room filled with amens as the congregation smiled while they listened. The bird's song caused Luke Yoder to give a silent denki to God for emphasizing his message. "Listen to the wren sing. He pleases us with his natural tune and has no more need for modern conveniences than we do. Now Bishop Bontrager will deliver his message." Luke returned to his seat.

Bishop Bontrager came forward. The fact that he focused on the boys toward the back of the room was not lost on Daniel. "Luke Yoder's message is very timely. I fear that too many of our youth in rumspringa have been tempted to buy a phone or a radio. Two items that are small enough to hide from parents. Take it from me if your parents do not find out, the more you think about your dishonesty to your parents, your faith and God, that alone will haunt you. Come forward and confess this sin and admit to wrong doing so God may forgive you.

Now I have been trying to decide what sermon to use for a special message. We are so blessed to be able to help each other in time of need. It is my feeling that we can endure any hardship put in our way as long as we have our church community to come to our aid. It is well for us to help others when the need arises, knowing some day we might need that help returned to us.

I have decided to talk about Paul's Request for Prayer this

morning. Paul prayed about some people's idle ways." Bishop Bontrager opened his bible and read, "He said to his brethren, "Now we command you, brethren, in the name of our Lord Jesus Christ, that ye withdraw yourselves from every brother that walketh disorderly, and not after the tradition which he received of us.

For yourselves, know how ye ought to follow us. For we behaved not ourselves disorderly among you. Neither did we eat any man's bread for naught; but wrought with labor and travail night and day, that we might not be chargeable to any of you.

Not because we have not power, but to make ourselves an example unto you to follow us. For even when we were with you, this we commanded you, that if any would not work, neither should he eat. For we hear there are some which walk among you disorderly, working not at all but are busybodies. Now them that are such we command and exhort by our Lord Jesus Christ, that with quietness they work, and eat their own bread.

But ye, brethren, be not weary in well doing. And if any man obey not our word by this epistle, note that man, and have no company with him, that he may be ashamed. Yet count *him* not as an enemy, but admonish *him* as a brother."

Bishop Bontrager looked around the congregation and settled his eyes on the the teenage boys again. "What was written in the bible reads so true still today. There are those among us that think to be busy bodies, as the bible calls them, when others are working hard to accomplish a task such as the Stolfus barn raising. When the hard working men were called to come break bread, the busy bodies came just as fast to sit among the workers for a share of the food. That was food they did not deserve since they did not work for it as Paul did. The busy bodies did not think anyone noticed them accept the food offering. Perhaps, not many around them took notice, but believe me when I say that what we on earth see and think is not as important as the fact that God was watching the busy bodies. It is him they will have to atone to for their sins.

139

You see Paul felt very strongly about laboring for the food he was to be given so he did not owe anyone for it. What did he tell his brethren? Not to get tired of well doing. Note the men who do not work as hard and have no company with them. For those men should be ashamed. We are not to count them as an enemy, but admonish them for their laziness as our brothers. Keep that in mind when we see the busy bodies among us.

Now time for the final hymn and prayer."

The bishop sat down, and Luke Yoder stood up. He picked Eli Mast to lead the last hymn. When that finished, Luke said the final prayer and announced, "Now Bishop Bontrager will come forward."

The bishop said, "There is a member meeting. All those that need to will leave the house now." After the younger generation left, the bishop said, "We are sadly missing a school that meant so much to many Plain generations as a place of learning and social gatherings.

Adam Keim has furnished a make shift school in the top of his store until a new school can be built. We are thankful for his coming forward so the pupils do not get too far behind in their learning.

Now we meet to determine when to erect the new school house and how much materials we will need. As soon as the fellowship meal is over, we should gather a committee to discuss this matter.

Does anyone have any other thoughts at this member meeting?"

Rudy Briskey stood up. "We sure hope the arsonist is caught soon, before anyone is killed in one of his fires. We have been lucky so far. Praise the Lord, Nurse Hal is all recht."

He was interrupted by the congregation with shouts of, "Amen!"

Rudy continued, "Each of the fires were an expense that costs dearly in our brotherly aid insurance fund. Without that fund, it would take some of us years to get over the loss of our property. More of the members need to think about paying their dues.

But for now to put money back in the fund to replace the barn expense and pay for the school house expense, we need to have a benefit frolic. It might be gute to have the women get in on that to give us ideas and help organize the benefit."

"That is gute. We have much to think about and work to do. I would say Paul would be pleased with us and think we are worthy of being fed. Now meeting adjourned so we can eat," Bishop Bontrager said and chuckled.

While Hal was serving the men their dessert, she set a piece of pumpkin pie by Rudy Briskey's plate. He looked up at her, concern on his face. "Nurse Hal, are you feeling all recht now?"

"Jah, I'm fine, Rudy," Hal said.

"I felt bad that the arsonist was in your barn when you had to go check the goat you bought from me," Rudy said contritely.

"Don't worry about it, Rudy." Hal turned to go back for another tray of pie. It surprised her that Rudy felt guilty about selling her a jumping goat that almost got her killed.

"Nurse Hal." She turned around. Rudy Briskey gave her that winning there's a sucker born every minute smile. "How is the milk goat doing now?"

Hal knew the complaints he expected to hear now that he knew she'd recovered, but he wouldn't get sour grapes from her. She looked across the table at John. He was glued to her every word, wondering how she'd handle the question. "Rudy, Gano is the friendliest, sweetest milk goat. The whole family has taken a liking to her. She's doing well with the sheep, too. She fits right in with them now. Denki so much for suggesting her to me." She glanced at John, and he winked at her.

Rudy's mouth gaped open.

Hal asked, "I have to finish helping serve the dessert. Were you going to say more, Rudy?"

"Nah, I am just glad the goat worked out so well," he said without his usual bluster.

"Denki so much. Everything about the goat is just fine for me. Even her name. I'd say for the Lapp family the name Gano is perfect. She's a *winner* all the way around as far as we're concerned. Well worth every bit of the bargain you gave us, Rudy." Hal whisk away before Rudy could speak.

As soon as the children walked out of the house, Daniel found Noah talking to Levi Yoder. Levi said, "Daniel, how are you this fine day?"

"Gute, and you?"

"I'm gute," Levi said.

Daniel put his hand on Noah's arm. "We need to talk."

"All recht, what is it?"

"Alone," Daniel said urgently.

Levi realized something was wrong. "I should go find out what time I am to pick my date up for the singing tonight. See you two there I reckon."

As soon as Luke was out of ear shot, Daniel said, "Come away from everyone where they cannot hear us." Noah followed. When they stopped, Daniel said, "The sermons today were aimed at you and me. I am sure of it. Have you listened to the radio lately?"

"Nah, I have not had the chance since I bought it, but there is not a way to know that me of all the boys has that radio. The sermons were for all of us. Your conscious is just bothering you," Noah excused.

"It is for a fact. Bishop Bontrager hit the nail on the head when he looked at me. I hate knowing you have a radio hid from Daed. When you have a chance, you should make sure that radio is still where you put it," Daniel insisted.

Chapter 13

During the fellowship luncheon, Wanda Bruner sat next to Hal. She fingered her silverware nervously.

Hal gave her a tentative smile. "How are you this fine day?"

"I am well enough. Praise the Lord!" Wanda exclaimed sheepishly and dropped her hands in her lap. She looked around to make sure the other women were busy eating or visiting with each other and said quietly, "Nurse Hal, I need to talk to you. My sister, Gladys, is not well. She is growing worse, and that is what worries me. She will not go to a doctor in Wickenburg for me, and I have asked often. Now part of the time she is out of her head with a high fever. I am very worried about her."

Hal sensed Wanda didn't want to ask for her medical help, but she needed Hal to offer because she was desperate. "Would you like me to make a house call to see Gladys?"

"Jah, I would feel better if I knew what was wrong with her. She is not getting any better, and this illness has gone on for days," Wanda said then added, "She has been in such an ill temper lately you must be careful when you are near her. She has hit me twice now when she has been out of her head with fever."

As soon as they finished lunch, Hal found Noah. She

asked him to hitch up their buggy for her. She whispered in John's ear where she was going and went to find her son-in-law, Adam Keim. "Adam, I need a favor."

His eyebrows went up, and his hand wobbled sideways.

"I need to make a house call on Wanda Bruner's sister. She's ailing. Could you and Emma take the family home when you're ready to leave if I'm not back in time? Wanda went to tell Enoch she's going with me so he has their buggy to get home."

Adam shook his head yes and waved his hand good bye at her.

In the quiet between them, Ben's rhythmic clopping sounded loud on the hard packed country road. To break the awkward silence, Hal asked, "How was the quilting bee Stella Strutt had?"

"Gute. Quilting bees frolics are always fun," Wanda said dully, staring at her lap.

"I agree. When we have one over my way, I will let you and Gladys know so you can come," Hal offered.

"Denki," Wanda said. She opened her mouth to say more than thought better of it.

"I get the feeling you're uneasy with me. You haven't any reason to be as far as I can see," Hal said quietly.

"I've heard many gute things about your nursing in the community," Wanda confirmed. "The bishop's wife speaks well of you."

"But," Hal glanced at Wanda for more. The woman's lips pinched shut. She wasn't going to add more. "I know there is a but in your mind. Let me guess what it is. Has Stella Strutt told you I own a car and cell phone?"

"Jah, she did," Wanda said shortly.

"Did Stella explain I can only use the car and phone for medical emergencies? I was given permission by the bishop and church members. Stella was there for the vote.

The church members recognize the advantage of having a way to reach the ambulance faster with my phone when I'm on the scene of a serious illness or accident. As long as I can use

144

my car I'm getting people to the hospital faster so they have a better chance of surviving. I've had many occasions to prove this to the Plain community."

"Stella Strutt does not see this like the others. She thinks you are breaking the Ordnung," Wanda said. "So do I."

"Stella doesn't have the final word. That decision was made at a member meeting and sanctioned by Bishop Bontrager.

Stella Strutt has not needed my medical help. She likes to complain about me. I think she'd sing a different tune if Moses or she were sick and needed me to help.

You should speak to some of the Plain people I've given medical aid to over the years," Hal asserted. "It's true you may find the permission to keep my car and phone isn't part of the Ordnung as you know it. It is what works in the Ordnung for this community. I do abide by the rule that I cannot use the car and phone for personal use. You can visit with the bishop about this. He will tell you the same thing," Hal said.

"All recht," Wanda replied quietly, watching the road in front of her.

"I don't wish to speak badly of Stella. Frankly, she feels she is the Plain Community's policeman as far as the Ordnung is concerned. She spends way too much time in council with Bishop Bontrager telling him her complaints. He takes what Stella tells him with a grain of salt until he investigates on his own. I don't know if you had noticed that about her."

Wanda smiled weakly and patted Hal's arm. "I noticed."

"I need to stop at my house to get my nursing bag out of the clinic to take with us," Hal said as she turned into the Lapp driveway.

Once they were on Bender Creek road, it wasn't much farther to the Bruner farm. Hal pulled in the driveway, drove close to the grossdawdi house and halted Ben.

Before Wanda opened the door, she cautioned, "I have to warn you Gladys will not like you coming here. I never know how she is going to react to strangers. She will be mad at me for disobeying her wishes about medical help."

145

"Don't worry. I am thick skinned. The main thing is we need to see if we can help your sister feel better," Hal told her.

Gladys's grossdawdi house set in the same yard as Wanda's home and was one large room. The kitchen was on one side, containing a small wooden table with a drop leaf to make it larger and two chairs next to a diminutive wood cookstove. A sink with a long drain board was under the window. On the other side the dining table was a small hutch filled with Wanda's china and glasses. The drawer under the shelves held her silverware.

Two rockers kept a small, round heating stove company in the middle of the room. On the other end of the house, hidden behind a quilt hung from the ceiling by wire, was a quarter size bed. The quilt was blue, black and purple squares in a round the world pattern. Beside the headboard were wall pegs holding black bonnets and dresses.

The house had a musky, sick smell like bedpan and unwashed, sweaty body combined. Gladys had been sick for some time. Hal slipped in behind Wanda and stood at the end of the bed. A commode was beside the bed. Along with the other odors, the house's stale air smelled of strong urine. Clearly, Gladys was too weak now to get out of bed to use the commode.

The pale, emaciated woman, in the bed, had her arm over her eyes.

Wanda said, "Sister, are you awake? I have brought the nurse to help you."

Gladys slowly removed her arm to look at Hal. Her feverish face was dry and flushed. Her lips cracked and bleeding.

Hal set her nursing bag on the floor and edged around the bed to get closer to her. "Gute afternoon, Gladys. I am Nurse Hal Lapp. It's nice to finally meet you."

The ill woman's face pinched tight and filled with hatred as she hissed weakly, "Get out of here, Englisher."

"I'm Amish just like you, and I won't stay long I promise," Hal said softly. "Your sister is very worried about you. She

146

asked me to check you to see if I can find out what's wrong with you." Hal put a hand on the woman's forehead.

The woman slapped her hand away but not before Hal felt her dry, feverish skin. Gladys's hands turned into claws as she flailed at Hal, trying to scratch her. "Do not lay your hands on me again."

Wanda's hands went to her blushing cheeks. "Awk, nah, sister. Stop that recht now. The nurse only wants to help you."

Hal held her hand up to interrupt. "It's all recht, Wanda. I'm done. Come to the kitchen with me so we can talk." Hal picked up her nursing bag and walked around the quilt.

Excited by anger, Gladys's chest heaved up and down in labored breathing. Hal heard very clearly loud wheezing and crackles coming from the woman's lungs. No need to try fighting her to listen to her lungs.

In the small kitchen as far away from the sick woman as they could get, Hal folded her arms across her chest and whispered, "Your sister has pneumonia. Whatever the reason, I can't determine it by looking at her. She really should go to the hospital in Wickenburg for tests. An x-ray on her lungs would help. The doctor will put her on an IV and antibiotics."

"She will not like to move, but I realize she cannot go on much long in this condition. Please, Nurse Hal, help my sister." Wanda's eyes glistened with desperation.

"I've done all I can. Gladys needs to go the hospital now," Nurse Hal said urgently, patting Wanda's arm.

If going to the hospital for tests is what she needs Enoch and I better take her," Wanda agreed as she listened to Gladys's labored breathing behind the curtain.

"Nah, that won't work. You need to let me call an ambulance. She's too weak to sit in a buggy. Besides, she needs the oxygen recht away an ambulance can provide to ease her breathing."

"I see. All recht, if you think that is best," Wanda agreed.

Hal asked, "She looks emaciated. Has she eaten much lately?"

Wanda pointed to the kitchen's one sink with a long

147

drainer. "Nothing for two days. All she does is drink orange juice."

About three dozen small, plastic bottles lined the back of the sink. "That's gute. At least, we can hope she isn't too dehydrated by the fever if she drank all those bottles of juice."

Wanda said, "Ach, she did not drink that many in the last few days. Gladys washes the bottles and saves them."

"Really. What does she do with them?" Hal asked.

"I do not know, but she insisted I wash up the last ones she drank just like she did. She has a reason I reckon. The number of bottles go down from time to time I notice. Gladys must throw a few away when the sink drain gets too crowded," Wanda said.

Hal put her hand on the woman's arm. "I carry the cell phone I talked about in my nursing bag. I can call the ambulance on that phone, but if you would rather I didn't use it, the phone booth is at the end of the mile. It will take more time to get the ambulance here when every minute might count for your sister as sick as she is. You tell me what you want me to do."

Wanda wrestled with the decision a moment. "If the whole community allows you to carry the phone, who am I to say nah especially when it is my sister that is so sick. Use your phone. You are recht. It will save time."

Wanda left the kitchen area. She carried a rocker to the end of the bed so she could watch her sister. Hal understood Wanda was willing to give into the phone to help her sister, but she didn't want to be guilty of being around when it was used.

Hal made the call. She requested the ambulance not use the siren. They should be told the patient is combative. Symptoms were a fever causing hallucinations, possible pneumonia and in need of oxygen.

Hal joined Wanda and nodded toward the bed. "Any change?"

"Nah, she is sleeping now," Wanda said.

Soon the Wickenburg ambulance pulled into the yard. Hal went out to greet the paramedics. Daryl slid out of the driver's seat. Steve came from the back, and Ivan got out on the passenger side.

"Hi, Nurse Hal. You're looking better than the last time we saw you," Daryl greeted, giving her his dead pan expression.

"I feel much better now. Thanks for getting me to the hospital all in one piece," Hal said, winking at Steve and Ivan.

Daryl grinned. "You're welcome. Now fill us in. We got from dispatch this is an uncooperative woman."

"Yes, the patient won't go willingly with you so you might need to restrain her on the gurney. She tried to hit and scratch me earlier," Hal warned. "She has pneumonia and a high temp. She's short of breath and needs oxygen. That might help keep her calm."

By that time, Ivan and Steve had the gurney by the porch steps. Steve waved a hand at the door. "Lead the way, Hal."

"I'll show you where she is, but I won't get where she can see me. She doesn't trust me, and my presence upsets her." Hal stopped the men by Wanda in the rocker. "This is Wanda Bruner, Gladys Kraybill's sister. She can answer your questions."

"Hi, Mrs. Bruner," Ivan said in a low voice, picking up the clipboard laying on the gurney. "How old is your sister?"

"Forty five," Wanda answered.

Ivan wrote the answer on the form. "How long has she been sick?"

Wanda looked toward the bed. "Maybe two weeks or a little more. Gladys isn't a complainer. She wasn't this sick to start with, but I couldn't get her to go to the doctor. Now she's much worse."

"We'll get her to the hospital," Steve said as he pulled the gurney after him. He touched the woman on the shoulder. "Gladys, can you hear me?"

The sick woman came unglued when she opened her eyes and found a strange man standing over her. "Get out of my bedroom. Wanda, help me. Where are you, Wanda?" She glared at Ivan and Daryl behind the gurney. "All of you. Get out of my house."

"Gladys, we're ambulance paramedics. We're going to take you to the hospital to see what's wrong with you," Steve said, edging toward her feet.

Ivan came to the middle of gurney and leaned over it toward the bed. Daryl went to the the head. He said in a quiet, calm tone, "At least let me cover you up better. Your arms will get cold uncovered like that." He brought the blanket up around her shoulders and tucked it gently behind her neck. He nodded at the other two men. "Now on three, covers and all. One, two, three. Lift!" He dodged to the end of the gurney, holding the struggling woman's shoulders while Steven and Ivan shifted her middle and feet. "Buckle her in tight," Daryl ordered.

Struggling and anxious, Gladys panted hard and screamed, "Let me go!"

The men pushed the gurney passed the curtain and turned it around on swiveling wheels. On the way down the porch steps, Gladys spotted Hal, standing by her buggy. She cried, "Do not believe anything that Englisher tells you. She is a liar."

Once the ambulance left the yard, Hal said, "Wanda, I always like to admit my patients and follow up at the hospital. I'll take you with me if you want to be with Gladys."

When they arrived at the hospital, Hal parked her buggy on the far side the parking lot and tied Ben to the hitching rail. The double doors shushed open when the women came close.

Nurse Lucy Stineford greeted Hal as they approached the nurse's desk. "Hi, Hal. We have your patient in an exam room. Dr. Christensen is with her."

"Is Gladys being difficult?" Wanda asked anxiously.

"Not right now," Lucy said crisply. She raised an eyebrow at Hal for who this woman was before she shared more private information.

Hal introduced Lucy to Wanda. "This is Gladys's sister. She has been Gladys Kraybill's caregiver. Can we see the patient?"

"Dr. Christensen has been waiting for you, Hal. He has questions," Nurse Lucy said. "Mrs. Bruner, can you stay here long enough to give me answers for my admittance form before you go to your sister?"

"Jah," Wanda said quietly, keeping her head bent with her face partially hidden under her bonnet brim.

"Thank you. Hal, follow me," Lucy said crisply. She stuck her head in the exam room door. "Doctor, I have the patient's sister at the desk and Nurse Hal with me."

Doctor Christensen looked up from writing on Gladys's chart. "Send the nurse in first."

"You need me for anything?" Nurse Lucy asked.

He shook his head. "Not right now. Go back to your paperwork."

"Hi, Doctor," Hal greeted quietly. Gladys seemed asleep, and Hal didn't want her to wake up and be combative right away. "You have any idea yet what's wrong with Gladys Kraybill? She has been sick for a couple weeks at least. Her sister couldn't get her to go to the doctor until we forced her today."

"She's very sick, and I can tell you the reason. How long ago did she get that nasty laceration on her leg?" Dr. Christensen asked.

"I didn't know about a laceration," Hal said in surprise.

Dr. Christensen looked puzzled.

"Don't look at me like that. The woman wouldn't let me near her while she's been sick. I don't think she was any more cooperative with her sister. She'd been trying to do everything for herself until the last day or two. Now she is too weak to help herself.

Today is the first time I've seen her. She slapped my hand away for feeling her forehead and ordered me out of her house. I heard the rattle in her chest and knew she had pneumonia. That was enough reason to send her to the emergency room, so I didn't try to argue with her about doing a complete exam," Hal explained. "I figured you could do that."

"Then you're in for a shock." The doctor lifted the sheet up from the bottom of the bed to expose Gladys's ankles and feet. "She has a contusion on that left ankle. The ankle is swelled

151

three times its normal size. From the green and yellow coloration, I'd say that has been there a week at least. I've ordered x-rays to see if the ankle is broken. What kind of an accident did this woman have?"

Hal shook her head slowly. "Gladys hasn't had an accident that I knew about. We need to ask her sister what kind of accident Gladys had when Lucy is done with her."

Hal walked to the foot of the bed for a closer look.

The doctor said, "That isn't the worse part. The worse part is the laceration on her leg." He pulled the sheet up to Gladys's knees.

Red streaks ran up the left thigh from the ankle. Yellow pus oozed from a jagged gash on the outer side of the leg. It was a foot long with scabbed over smaller punctured spots around it.

Hal was mystified. "I didn't know about any of this. Like I said she wouldn't let me near her. Talk to her sister."

The doctor pushed a button on the intercom attached to the wall. "Lucy, bring the patient's sister to the exam room."

The exam door opened, and Lucy stepped in with Wanda. "This is the patient's sister, Wanda Bruner," she told the doctor.

"Come in, Mrs. Bruner," he said. "We need more information about your sister."

"I'll tell you anything I can," Wanda said softly.

Hal took her hand. "Come over to the bed and look at Gladys's left leg. She has hurt it very badly recently. Did she mention an accident to you?"

"Nah, she didn't." Wanda stopped by the bed. When she saw the gangrenous wound she clamped her hand over her mouth. She looked away while she regained her composure before she spoke. "No wonder she has been in pain and sick."

The doctor explained, "The wound is old and has been left untreated. The leg is infected. Full of gangrene. I'll clean the wound, but we might not be able to save her leg. For that matter, not her either now that she has infection through her system. Of course, I'll do what I can. The rest is up to her."

"And God," Wanda added.

152

"Did the paramedics tell you Wanda was combative?" Hal asked the doctor. "She definitely will pull out the IV tube when she comes around."

Dr. Christensen nodded. "Lucy and I saw that for ourselves. I ordered a sedative given to her to calm her down. "Now we wait to see how well the IV works. Hopefully, we see some improvement by morning. She's going to be moved to Intensive Care right away."

Wanda said, "I want to stay with my sister until I know she is feeling better."

"That's fine. The patient might be more cooperative if she has you with her," Doctor Christensen said as he went out the door.

"I'm going home, so I'll stop and update Enoch. Wanda, is Gladys a good horseman?" Hal asked.

"At one time, she was, but she had given up on life a long time ago. I have not seen her ride in years. You might as well know her thinking has been all crooked and bitter. She grew worse each time she heard one of her lifetime friends had switched to Beachy Amish. Why do you want to know about her riding a horse?"

Hal replied offhandedly, "Ach, I just wondered if Gladys fell off a horse recently. Maybe that was how she got hurt."

Worried, Wanda stared at her very ill sister. "Nah, she has not been on one."

Hal had a feeling about the shape of the wound on Gladys's leg. Could it have been her blood left on the Stolfus barbed wire fence? The arsonist used small juice jugs to carry kerosene. The fact Gladys's drainboard was laden with plastic juice bottles seemed like a peculiar coincidence. The thought wouldn't leave Hal's head. Gladys Kraybill might be the arsonist. Could Enoch and Wanda have slept through her nightly excursions?

Hal wasn't going to feel right about being aware all this information until she reported what she knew to the sheriff.

Chapter 14

Right away Hal drove to the sheriff's office. She asked at the desk to speak to Sheriff Dawson. He came to his office doorway. "I thought I recognized your voice, Mrs. Lapp. Listen, if you're here about information on the school fire, I haven't any lines on who did it yet."

"Nah, I am here, because I might know who set all the fires," Hal admitted.

The sheriff looked surprised. "Come in my office and tell me. I'm all ears."

After they were seated, Hal explained, "I just helped admit an Amish patient at the hospital ER. The woman has a long, jagged gash on the outside her lower left leg and a very swollen ankle, possibly broken, with at least two weeks old bruising or maybe longer.

Her name is Gladys Kraybill. She moved here from Kansas recently with her sister, Wanda Burner and Wanda's husband, Enoch. They have been in the Plain community such a short time I hadn't met Gladys until today. Her sister, Wanda, told us she has been too sick to come to worship services. Her sister says the woman has been depressed and bitter about so many Plain people she knew where they lived before becoming Beachy Amish. Not a pleasant person for her family to be around I gather."

"I expect you see all sorts of wounds from farm injuries," Sheriff Dawson said, leaning forward in his chair and placing his elbows on the desk. "What makes you think this one is suspicious?"

"I might not have if I hadn't seen about three dozen cleaned small, plastic juice bottles on the woman's kitchen sink drainboard. According to Wanda, Gladys drinks a lot of orange juice and keeps the bottles. Her sister doesn't know why she saved them, but she knew that the amount of bottles on the drainboard goes down times. Wanda assumed Glady threw some of the bottles away."

"Interesting," the sheriff said, sitting up straight in his chair.

"Add to that the fact that Wanda says the woman is a good horse rider, but she doesn't think Gladys has been on a horse for years. Of course, the arsonist strikes in the middle of the night when Wanda and her husband are asleep.

I thought maybe while the woman is in the hospital you might get Dr. Christensen to order a blood test to compare with your DNA sample from the Stolfus fence. Now would be an easy time to get a finger print, too. Gladys Kraybill is sedated to keep her from fighting and pulling out the IV tube."

"You think she will be in the hospital long?" The sheriff asked.

"Dr. Christensen is admitting her to Intensive Care. He says she might not recover. She should have seen a doctor right away with a wound like that especially if it was made by rusty barbed wire. She has never had a tetanus shot. If she setting a barn on fire when she got hurt, that might be the reason she was so adamant about not going to the doctor.

Her body is full of infection. If she lives, it's a good possibility she will loose her leg," Hal told him. "Sheriff, I'd rather you not tell anyone you got her health information from me. I'm not supposed to tell any of this because of patient confidentiality health privacy."

"I understand. Do you think her sister and brother-in-law were involved in this and trying to cover up for her?"

"If I'm right about Gladys being guilty, I'm pretty sure the family didn't know what she'd done. Wanda said she hadn't seen Gladys ride a horse, and she was puzzled about why her sister kept the juice bottles. As cranky as Gladys is, I think Wanda kept her questions to herself to keep the confrontations down."

"Do you know where in Kansas the family came from? It might be a good idea to check on this woman's past," the sheriff said. "If she had the law suspicious of her there that might be why the family moved."

Hal paused. "I think I heard Hutchinson, Kansas mentioned."

Sheriff Dawson asked, "So you and Emma Keim have given up on Albert Jostle as our suspect?"

Hal shrugged. "I don't know. I could be wrong about Gladys. Did you find out anything about Albert?"

"I did. It's probably the reason for their move here from the Amish community near Middleton in Minnesota. Albert and a deacon's son were arrested for being Peeping Toms. Since they were only thirteen, the boys were released into the custody of their parents. It didn't take the Jostle family long to move to Wickenburg out of the reach of harassment."

Hal's forehead furrowed. "Ack, nah! Emma sure had Albert pegged. She sensed that boy might be a pervert. So it wouldn't take much for him to go from peeking in windows to setting a building on fire."

"I was thinking the same thing," Sheriff Dawson agreed.

Hal stood up. "If I am right about Gladys Kraybill, I'm sure the whole county will sleep better knowing you caught the arsonist, but I'm not sure how the Amish Community will treat the family of the guilty person."

"No need for me to bring what you told me out in the open right now. We have to investigate first before we accuse either Kraybill or Jostle and see where that leads us. I do thank you for coming in with this information," the sheriff said. "You're making my job easier."

"You're wilcom. Now I have to go by the Bruner farm to

tell Enoch what's going on with his sister'-in-law. His wife wanted to stay with her sister tonight so he needs to know Wanda isn't coming home until tomorrow."

On the way home, Hal worried about what she suspected about Gladys Kraybill. She certainly didn't want to discuss the woman with Enoch. This was something she wanted to discuss with John and let him help her decide if she should talk to the bishop.

The milk generator was humming by the time Hal reached home. She'd just have to wait until after supper to talk to John. The boys were going to the youth singing. She'd have John alone to tell him about Gladys Kraybill and Albert Jostle.

Hal peeled potatoes and set the pan on the stove. Maybe some sausage cakes would go good with potatoes and gravy. Hal headed for the basement to bring back the jars of sausage. A jar of carrots caught her eye so she grabbed it, too.

Soon Hal had the stove filled with pans, and the cakes sizzling in the skillet. While she was turning the sausage cakes, she heard the front door open.

"Hello, you in here, Hallie?" Emma called.

"In the kitchen," Hal shouted. Emma appeared in the doorway. "I didn't hear you drive in. Adam with you?"

"He headed for the barn. Can I help you fix supper?"

"Jump right in anywhere you want," Hal declared.

"The house is quiet. Where are the girls?" Emma asked as she checked the skillets and kettle on the stove.

"They must be in the barn with the men. I got home from the hospital rather late," Hal said as she looked out the window toward the barn.

Emma asked, "You want me to make a pan of biscuits to go with the sausage and gravy?"

Hal didn't answer. She was still staring out the window with a far away look on her face.

"Hallie?" Emma didn't get a response so she walked over and patted Hal on the shoulder. "Hallie, are you all recht?"

Hal flinched with surprise. "Ach! Of course, I'm all recht. Why?"

"I have been talking to you, and you didn't hear me. Something happened today after you left with Wanda Bruner that bothers you, ain't so?"

"Jah, and after supper, I need to discuss it. I'd like Adam and John to be here when I do," Hal said. "Now did you say something important that I missed?"

"I wondered if you want me to put a pan of biscuits in the oven for supper to go with the sausage and gravy?"

Hal laughed. "Sure enough, that was important. Of course, you must make us some of your light, flaky biscuits."

After supper and devotion was over, the boys left for the singing. Emma said, "Now, Hallie, out with it. I am very curious."

Adam's eyebrows raised at John.

"I do not know what this is about, Adam. So is something wrong, Hal?" John asked.

Hal nodded. "In the English world as Gladys Bruner's nurse, I'm not supposed to talk about her health or anything concerning her. What I've found out today is too much of a burden for me to keep to myself. I need my family to tell me what to do next."

John asked, "How is Gladys Kraybill?"

Hal said, "Very ill. Wanda stayed to be with her, but Gladys doesn't know that or anything else. Hopefully, by morning Gladys's health will improve or worsen."

"What is it about Gladys that worries you?" Emma asked.

"After I saw her infected leg wound, found she drinks orange juice in small bottles and saves the plastic bottles, I got to thinking she might be the arsonist. So I went to the sheriff to report Gladys and tell him this would be a gute time to get a sample of her blood for DNA. If that sample matches the blood on the Stolfus fence, she's the arsonist. Now do I keep quiet about this investigation so people aren't hard on the Bruners? Enoch and Wanda cannot help what Gladys did if she's guilty."

John rubbed the back of his neck. "This seems like a problem for Bishop Bontrager to handle. I think people would breathe easier if they knew the arsonist is not going to strike again. If the woman lives, we have to wait to see what the sheriff finds out. If he arrests her, everyone will know anyway."

"Enoch and Wanda just moved here. They are gute people, and I hate to see anyone be unkind to them," Emma said.

"What do you think, Adam?" Hal asked.

Adam pointed at Emma and patted his chest. He believed as she did.

"If Gladys dies, it seems a shame to reveal she did these awful things. It would be better for the Bruners if people didn't know," Hal said.

"That is true," Emma agreed. "Just think, I was ready to blame Albert Jostle for the fires."

"Ach, I almost forgot. Sheriff Dawson found out that Albert had been charged with window peeking. That is why his family moved here and are so withdrawn around us. They want to hide what Albert did," Hal shared.

"I was afraid the sheriff would find out something like that, but as long as Albert behaves himself, we have to hope he has changed his ways," Emma said.

While the boys unhitched Ben from the buggy that evening, Daniel said, "You are very quiet tonight."

Noah said, "I have been thinking about the radio."

"Did you look to make sure the radio is still hidden on the rafter while we milked?"

"Nah, I didn't, but I will while we are out here alone."

Daniel took Ben's lead rope. "Gute, go do that while I take Ben to the pasture gate."

When Daniel came back, Noah leaned against the barn with his hands stuffed in his pockets. "Well?"

Noah's voice trembled. "The radio is gone."

"I was afraid of that. I have a feeling the radio did not just disappear. Daed has found it," Daniel said.

"I am afraid of that, too," Noah said softly.

"You better talked to him recht away, before he has to confront you. He will go easier on you that way," Daniel

159

insisted.

When they entered the house, Hal was reading the latest issue of Family Life. John had the Wickenburg Daily in front of his face.

Hal greeted, "Ach, back already. How fast the evening flies."

Both boys nodded at her and put their hats on their pegs.

Hal's forehead wrinkled in concern as she tried again, "Did you have a gute time?"

"Jah," Daniel answered. "We had a gute time."

Noah cleared his throat as he stepped from one foot to the other. "Daed?"

John lowered the newspaper. "Jah?"

"Could we talk in the kitchen? I have something to tell you," Noah said.

"Sure enough." John laid the newspaper beside the rocker and stood up.

Noah followed his father and sit across the table from where John sat down. "I have something to confess to you."

"I see." John stuck his hand in his trouser pocket and slipped out the radio. "Would it happen to be about this radio I found in the loft?"

"I'm not surprised. When I found it gone, I knew you must have it. The sermon today was aimed at me, wasn't it?"

"Not just you. Was Daniel a part of this? Maybe he should be in here, too," John said sternly.

"Nah, he tried to talk me out of buying the radio, and I would not listen to him. That radio has been on the rafter for awhile, and I have been too busy to listen to it," Noah said.

"That is gute. You have found your life is just as well off without a radio, but why did you buy it in the first place?"

"Albert Jostle and some of the other boys in rumspringa said they liked their radio. They thought it was a gute idea if I had one," Noah excused.

"Even though you knew better. By buying this English convenience, you have tested the boundaries to the limit. You knew you were breaking the Ordnung. I raised you to know our faith prohibits all things modern.

I'm glad you came to me on your own. I was not going to wait much longer to confront you. Are you sorry you bought the radio?"

"Jah, my conscious has been bothering me ever since I put the radio in my pocket. I am sorry for being so dishonest," Noah said tearfully.

"That is gute. I cannot let this transgression go without some sort of punishment. You are to stay home from the youth singing for the next two Sundays. I am going to get rid of the radio, and we will not talk about this again," John said.

"Denki, Daed." Now that the confession was over Noah let out a whooshing sigh of relief.

John stood and stuffed the radio back in his trouser pocket. "How about we call it a night. We have work to do tomorrow."

The next evening, John and Hal visited Bishop and Jane Bontrager so Hal could tell the bishop what she found out about Gladys Kraybill.

The elderly couple were surprised. They hadn't met Gladys, but they were well enough acquainted with the Bruners to wonder how Gladys could be so different from them.

Elton agreed with Hal that it wouldn't hurt to keep quiet about their suspicions until Gladys was officially charged. He asked Nurse Hal to keep him posted.

As Jane poured them each a cup of coffee, Elton asked John if Sunday's sermon had rendered gute results. John grinned and nodded. He told Elton that Noah came forward on his own and confessed. He found the radio was missing from the rafter, and his guilty conscious had him thinking the sermon was meant just for him. Some of the boys in rumspringa persuaded Noah to buy the radio. Once he hid it on the rafter, he'd been too busy to listen to it so he came to the conclusion he really didn't need it anyway.

Elton told John he was glad the sermon had been so successful. He just wished the boys in other households were as easy to convince as Noah was.

161

Chapter 15

One buggy after the other lined up on the way to a benefit frolic fund raiser. Money was needed to replace what was used for a list of recent debts such as for the Stolfus barn raising, the future schoolhouse raising, plus Nurse Hal and Gladys Bruner's hospital stay. What money was left over would be stay in the fund for later emergencies.

Levi Yoder furnished his hay field for the event. Buggies and car parking was in the pasture across the road.

In early October, Luke placed a sign along side the road in front of his farm indicating a Benefit Frolic would be held. More signs, with the date and address of the benefit, were placed on the edge of the four pavements going into Wickenburg.

This was quite an undertaking for the Amish community. Second only to the Stolfus barn raising. Everyone donated something whether it be an item for the auction, food or apples for the bobbing game. The committee made out a work list for each of the events. When the volunteers weren't working, they could enjoy the frolic.

On Saturday, everything was in place for the benefit. Plain people arrived early to work. Amish men directed the traffic into the pasture driveway and to the spot in line to park.

Some visitors hadn't heard about the benefit, but as they

drove by, they were curious about the tent and booths. They wondered what such a large gathering of Amish were up to so they stopped.

A minor traffic jam developed on the road as people arrived. Visitors climbed out of their cars, and walked across the road. Hundreds stood in line waiting their turn to go through the hay field gate hole. The fee was five dollars for the day for adults and two dollars for children fourteen and over. Admission included meals and games for all ages.

Ben trotted down the road early that morning, pulling the Lapp family buggy. John and Hal were eager to get to the frolic to help. Noah and Daniel looked forward to a day of fun with their friends. Redbird and Beth were too young to understand what all the excitement was about, but they would enjoy playing with children their age.

A red sport car, containing a thoughtless driver, raced past the Lapp buggy and others in the parade headed for the Yoder farm. The young blond man laid his hand on the horn, warning the Plain people to stay out of his way. Luckily, the well behaved horses were used to cars and just kept trotting as the dust fogged the air.

Once inside the gate, English and Amish milled around wondering where they should start. It was suddenly clear why the Amish were so committed to their faith. Where else could you find a community that would put together such a work intensive benefit to help others pay their expenses?

Several days before the event, Amish gathered to ready the hay field. They put up a large blue and white tent for resting and eating meals in. Benches, normally for the worship services in the home, would be put together in the tent as tables and seats. Places for the many visitors sit and eat lunch and later for the auction crowd. The dish chests were stacked in one corner of the tent.

Sawhorses with boards across them lined both sides the tent. These were laden with various items. At one end of a plank were delicious Eve Weber's homemade pretzels. On the other end was Roseanna Nicely's doughnuts mound on platters.

163

For lunch, the planks on the other side the tent held the buffet. The smell of barbecue chicken filled the air. Ham and cheese sandwiches piled high beside stainless steel pans of baked beans and potato salad. For dessert, several cakes were on the end.

Eve Weber, the tall, thin one of the Weber sisters, was in charge of the food. She liked to talk and kept up a running conversation with the diners, making strangers feel welcome.

At lunch time, people, ready to rest, put food on their paper plates, filled a Styrofoam cup with tea or coffee and sit down to eat. While the diners ate, teenagers sang hymns for them. The teenagers divided in to singing groups of six to sing for thirty minutes. They had plenty of practiced singing every Sunday night and enjoyed entertaining the lunch crowd. Noah and Daniel were with the first group.

As soon as the Lapp brothers finished singing, they headed for the wiener roast. Just before noon, the bond fire was lit. Children interested in the hot dog and marshmallow roast could partake of that instead of the food tent. Sticks to spear the hot dogs were piled by a cooler full of hot dogs. A cardboard box was filled with sacks of large marshmallows. Coolers of grape Kool Aide and cups to hold the drinks were stacked on a folding table.

In the close cut clover, enough bases for two softball diamonds were marked with a small square of lime. The two winning teams would play in the play off game. Two nets were put up for a volleyball tournament. The teams might be a mixture of Amish and English or a team of each. One area was horseshoe games for the men. The log sawing contest gathered a crowd to watch three different cross saws inch through large logs. For the elder males in the crowd, checker boards had been set up on folding tables.

All day long, younger children bobbed for apples. Red delicious apples floated in six tubs. It was quite a challenge for the participants to sink their teeth into an apple that dived under water at the slightest touch.

Taffy pulls were another part of the fun. Roseanna Nisely

place a cast iron kettle over a small fire. She had the molasses taffy syrup boiled to its hard ball stage and spread on cookie sheets on a folding table just as the first children reached her. She handed each pair of pullers a piece of the cooled taffy the size of a softball and told them to see who could get their taffy ready first. When the taffy color changed to a golden brown, it was too hard to pull.

The children laid the taffy on a sheet for Roseanna to cut in pieces. The children ate what they wanted and moved on. Baking sheets of taffy pieces were left for grownups and other children who had been in another event.

Small square pens in one area were a petting zoo, holding small animals like lambs, goats, calves, kittens, rabbits and puppies for the younger children. Emma offered to watch Redbird and Beth while Hal worked in the food tent. The first place she took the girls was to the petting zoo. The girls weren't as impressed by the baby animals as the English children were. They saw these animals every day at home, In a few moments, they were ready to move on.

Next Emma took the girls to the pony rides in a small roped in arena. She put both girls on a small black and white paint pony's back and led the pony in a circle. The girls thought that was fun. The ponies were closer to the ground than the Lapp horses. Everyone was so busy at home no one took the time to help Redbird and Beth ride bareback. Emma made a mental note to tell Daed by the girls' birthday, a pony would be the ideal gift.

On the second time around, a man said, "Looks like the girls are having fun."

Emma glanced at the young blond man with his arms cross on top of the fence posts for the rope corral. "Jah," she answered and kept moving. She wondered where she had seen this man before.

On the next circle around the corral, he was still there. She glanced over, and he smiled at her. It was then Emma remembered. The man drove a fancy red sports car to the benefit. He sped past all the buggies like he owned the road.

165

"The girls your children?" He asked as his bright blue eyes inspected her.

Emma's instincts told her this was not a man to get friendly with. "Nah."

She walked on. When she had the girls on the opposite of the corral from the man, she helped the girls down with the promise to go have taffy candy.

A wash tub was full of molasses. Beside the tub was a small table holding plates of biscuits. Anyone with a taste for molasses dipped pieces of biscuits and got sticky until they had eaten their fill. Boxes of wet ones on the table were to wipe the sticky molasses from hands and lips, before they moved on to the next event.

If frolic goers hadn't eaten enough at lunch there was a help yourself dessert booth with a counter full of various pie and cake pieces on paper plates and stacks of paper cups to fill from cold tea, lemonade and coffee coolers.

Bashful, heavy set Esther Weber was in charge of setting up the booth. Her sister, Eve Weber, left the clean up in the lunch tent to other women. She made it to the dessert booth in time to help Esther replace saucers in the empty spots on the counter. A diesel engine putt-putted turning an ice cream machine, making homemade ice cream to top off the desserts.

Noah appeared in the food tent juggling two piece of apple pie topped with ice cream and two cups of tea. He searched the crowd, looking for Jenny Yoder. She had just finished her dish washing shift. He winked at her which made her blush as she came to meet him.

"Want to share my apple pie and ice tea?" Noah asked.

Jenny wiped her damp forehead with her apron. "That sounds gute. Doing dishes is hot work. There is not one bit of air in that corner of the tent."

"That big maple tree in your yard is a cool shady spot. Come on," Noah said.

After they sat down, Noah pulled the forks out of his shirt pocket and gave Jenny one. "We better eat fast. The ice cream is melting."

166

Jenny took a bite from her saucer and said, "This is gute. It hits the spot."

"I'm glad," Noah said. "Jenny, I have something to tell you." He grimaced, not wanting to say more.

"All recht, what is it?"

"I will not be able to take you to the next two singings," he said.

Jenny looked at Noah over her cup as she took a sip of tea. She propped the cup against her leg on the unleveled ground. "That is not a problem. I can get there on my own, but why?"

"It is my punishment to stay home for buying a radio and hiding it from Daed. He found it, and now I am in trouble."

"I see. This surprises me. I might expect something like this from Daniel, but you are usually the one that makes wise decisions. What made you buy a radio?"

Noah sighed. "Albert Jostle and some of the other boys were at the salebarn. Albert said he had a radio and he liked it. So I bought one. I hid it in the hay loft. Daed found it, and I am in trouble. In all the time I had that radio, I did not find a moment to go to the loft to listen to it."

Jenny frowned. "Ach, and what does that tell you about having an English convenience?"

"I did not need it in the first place," Noah answered, staring in his empty cup to avoid looking at her.

Jenny leaned over and put her hand on Noah's arm. "That is recht. Be glad your father did not make your punishment worse than missing two singings. The time will go fast, and you come get me on the third Sunday."

In one booth, along the back, items for sale ranged from a pile of quilts, carved wooden knickknacks, canned jams and farm fresh eggs. Noah and Daniel donated part of their butternut and acorn squash and pie pumpkin harvest.

English customers bought baked goods, dressed chickens, souvenirs and jams. Amish food had a reputation far and wide from Wickenburg, Iowa. English people were always hungry for baked goods and jams.

Even the buggies the Amish arrived in received a great

167

deal of attention from out-of-state visitors. They couldn't resist lining up for the buggy rides or peeking into some of the parked buggies to see what the insides looked like.

After lunch, the grownups went to the auction in the food tent. Items for sale were jellies and jams, quilts, hand made wooden furniture, tools, birdhouses and other lawn ornaments. All the Amish donated at least one item. Some of the wooden pieces were made by Adam Keim.

During the day, Luke Yoder talked to many of the visitors and thanked them for coming. He was asked more than once how the benefit came to be on his farm. He'd stroke his beard as he related that Bishop Bontrager and John Lapp asked him to host, because his pasture was an ideal location and large enough for the benefit frolic. His hay field across the road was handy for plenty of parking. "That's how I ended up getting involved. I owned the land convenient for the benefit frolic."

Luke Yoder, as a Amish ambassador of good will, was a more valuable help with more than just donating his the land for the day. He enjoyed wandering through the crowd, visiting with people, and making sure things went smoothly. He wanted everyone to enjoy themselves as much as he did.

When people talked to Bishop Elton Bontrager, he said John Lapp and he picked a farm with the right location for the benefit, and God picked them a gute day. Everyone he mentioned the gute day to agreed with him. People from many different backgrounds and places mingled together. They had fun and supported a good cause, but most of them probably didn't even know what that cause was.

At the fund raiser frolic were several generations in the same families, from grandparents to grandchildren, who had all come together to work to replenish the Amish emergency fund. As is the case with these kinds of frolics, whether Amish or not, there's a great deal of work, but also a lot of joy felt by all the Amish because of a job well done.

168

Chapter 16

The last visit Hal made to the hospital, Gladys looked close to death. She had been moved from ICU to a room on one of the wards while the doctor waited to see some improvement in her condition.

While Hal was with Wanda, Sheriff Dawson came in. He removed his hat. "Mrs. Bruner, could I speak with you a moment about your sister?"

"Why?" Wanda asked, her senses dulled from lack of sleep and worry.

"I know this isn't a good time, but I haven't got a choice." He took a closer look at Gladys and made the same assessment Hal did when she came in the room. "Did you know your sister set those three fires in the Amish community?"

"Nah, that can not be so," Wanda cried.

The agony in her voice made Gladys squirm and flinch.

The sheriff said quietly, "I know it must be hard to believe, but Dr. Christensen gave me a blood sample from the wound on your sister's leg. I got a sample from Jonah Stolfus's barbed wire fence where the arsonist caught a leg on the barbs. I had the lab compare the samples. They match.

Each of fires were set with juice bottles filled with kerosene. I just came from your sister's house. Your husband let me in to look around. I found the juice bottles on the kitchen counter your sister saved. They match the fragments from the fire sights. There isn't any doubt in my mind that your sister is guilty," Sheriff Dawson said. "From the length of time Dr. Christensen estimated she's had the wound his findings coincides with the barn burning. All the evidence points toward your sister as the arsonist."

"Ach, nah," cried Wanda.

Hal took her hand and squeezed it as the sheriff asked, "Any idea why she wanted to do something that terrible? You just moved here. Your sister didn't have a chance to get to know anyone well enough to want to cause them harm or do damage to their property."

Wanda looked dazed. "I cannot answer that. You are recht. She did not know anyone except for what I told her about people when I came back from Sunday worship services."

"Can you remember anything you told Gladys about the Stolfus family, Rudy Briskey or the schoolhouse?" Hal asked.

"After one Sunday service, I told Gladys Freda Stolfus was one woman I met. I said she was nice. Later after I talked to Stella Strutt she told me the story about Jonah Stolfus shooting the young girl. I mentioned to Gladys what Stella told me Gladys said the man should not have been set free after committing murder.

Another time, I talked about how generous the neighbors were to help Jonah Stolfus rebuild his barn. Enoch and I were looking forward to the barn raisin' frolic. Oh, my!" Wanda stared at her sleeping sister.

"What is it, Wanda?" Hal asked.

"I told Gladys that Rudy Briskey offered Jonah Stolfus a whole load of hay to put in the loft. That generous offer spurred others to donate hay, too. I remember Gladys got the most hateful look on her face."

"What do you suppose she had against the school?" Sheriff Dawson asked.

Wanda thought a moment. "I told her Nurse Hal was the school teacher's step-mother."

Hal was surprised. "Why would that bother Gladys?"

"Stella Strutt told me you had a cell phone and car like the Beachy Amish in Kansas. Stella said you were English, and you converted to Amish when you married John Lapp.

I shared that with Gladys. She said you would always cause trouble and get the Plain people to change to Beachy Amish so you could use your phone and car. You were not of our kind since you were English through and through. Marrying John Lapp could not make you Amish. She told me to wait and see.

I tried to explain your duties as a nurse were needed. Your family was well respected in the community. I am so sorry, Hal. I didn't realize my conversations with my sister would cause so much trouble. I was just trying to get her familiar with people in the community so when she was well enough to join us at the worship services she'd already know something about the congregation."

"Ma'am, one more thing you should know, I talked to the sheriff where you came from in Kansas. He told me in recent years there had been several fires set around the county. He didn't have a clue who did it, but the fires stopped right before you left Kansas. I can't say for sure, but I expect your sister was setting those fires. She unhappy with people where you lived?"

"Jah, she was, because they were changing to Beachy Amish so they could live with modern conveniences like the English do. That is why we moved here. So we could be in an Old Order Amish community," Wanda said. "What are you going to do to my sister?"

"Just so you know we might as well let this information be between us for right now unless you want to tell folks what your sister did. Don't look like she's going to live long enough to be prosecuted for the crime. If she did improve, I'd have to arrest her."

"Denki, Sheriff. I am sorry for my sister's grave actions," Wanda implored.

After the sheriff left, Hal said, "We can all breath a sigh of relief now that there won't be anymore fires. That is a blessing."

"Hal, you are recht, but I am afraid of what everyone will think of Enoch and me if they find out what Gladys did. They might blame Enoch and me, too," Wanda worried. "After all, they do not know us very gute yet."

Hal thought Wanda might be right. "Well, we can wait for awhile and let people calm down. Perhaps, we wouldn't have to say anything. No more fires, and after while people will stop thinking about the arsonist. Life will go back like usual."

"I'd like that. At least until the Plain community gets to know Enoch and me," Wanda told her.

Hal waited two days, thinking she'd hear Gladys Kraybill had passed away. When she didn't hear from Wanda, she went back to the hospital. The intensive care room was empty. Hal asked the nurse where the patient was. She said Gladys had improved enough she'd been taken to surgery to remove her leg.

A few hours later, Gladys was back in intensive care. The pale woman was unresponsive and hooked to machines. The nurse said she couldn't have company except for her sister.

Sheriff Dawson had left a request to be kept informed on her condition. A few days later, Gladys moved to a room on the ward. Hal was sitting with Wanda when the sheriff came in.

"Howdy, ladies. How is Miss Kraybill doing?" He asked Wanda.

"She is in and out of sleep right now, but the doctor says she should continue to improve," Wanda said dully.

"In a few days when the woman is conscious and understands what I'm telling her, I'll be back," he said and left.

The day the sheriff was told by the nurse that Gladys was doing better and might be released soon, he drove out to visit Hal. "I want you there when I go in Gladys Kraybill's room. The doctor says it will be awhile before the stump heals. She needs to be confined and nursed. Then will come physical therapy with a crutch and to strengthen her arms so she can get herself out of bed and into a wheelchair. The doctor says he will let her go home to mend if you take over as the Home

Health nurse."

"Is that the way you want it?" Hal asked.

"It's a sure bet the woman isn't going to flee in the shape she's in. If her sister is willing to take her back home, I think the law can be patient. When she is healed and strong enough, I will arrest her."

"I see. Do you want me to go with you now?"

"If you don't mind," the sheriff said.

Gladys looked at the sheriff stoned faced while he told her she was under house arrest until she mended. As soon as her leg healed and her strength returned, he'd arrest her and take her to jail. Her expression changed when the doctor said Nurse Hal Lapp was going to be her home health nurse to tend her wound and help her with therapy. The woman glared at Hal. Sheriff Dawson said she had to abide by what they told her to do, or she could go to jail right away and suffer in a prison hospital bed.

The next morning, Hal and Wanda arrived to take Gladys home. She patted Wanda's hand and mustered up a smile for her, but she eyed Hal distastefully. Nurse Lucy came in and helped Hal transfer Gladys to a wheelchair to take her to the car.

Wanda helped with Gladys transfer from Hal's car to the wheelchair.

"Gute job," Hal encouraged.

"If you say so." Gladys tone was snide.

Wanda spoke with slow exactness. "Sister, you must remain polite and accept our help as Sheriff Dawson wanted you to do."

"Jah, I am sorry,sister," Gladys said contritely.

A month later, the sheriff came to check on Gladys. "You look like you getting around well enough in that wheelchair. I'm going back to town and talk to the doctor. If he's willing to release you in my custody, tomorrow morning I'll be out to arrest you."

Wanda sat through the visit tight lipped and with tears in

her eyes.

As soon as the sheriff left, Gladys said, "No need to feel sorry for me, sister. Feel sorry for yourself when the Plain community finds out it was one of your kin that started the fires. Life here will not be easy for Enoch and you."

Wanda saw to it that Gladys was in bed early that night. On retrospective, she'd later remember Gladys was the most peaceful and docile she'd seen her sister in years.

Gladys reached out and grasped Wanda's hand. "Denki for all you have done for me. I am most grateful for your help and thankful that you are my sister. I pray God will forgive me for the wrong I have done to you and to others."

Wanda left the grossdawdi house puzzled by the change in Gladys. Surely, this meant Gladys had made peace with herself and God. She seemed accepting and ready for what was to come in the morning when the sheriff came to take her to jail.

Wanda slowly climbed her porch steps, feeling sad for her sister and hating to see morning come. It startled her when a mourning dove flew off the arm of one of the three rockers lined up on the porch. With apprehension, Wanda realized the dove had been perched on Gladys's rocker. Wanda watched as the bird circled over the grossdawdi house three times before flying away. That bird usually brought some sort of bad warning when it came close to people. Surely, nothing any worse than what was going to happen in the morning could happen.

Tick tock, tick tock. The steady grinding of the tiny wheels inside the alarm clock by the bed penetrated the dark quiet of the room. Gladys listened for a few minutes, before she fold her hands together and prayed, "This is not Thy will, God, but I have lived as long as I can in the shape I am in. I do not plan to spend any time behind bars. I will not ever be wilcom in this community after the trouble I have caused. Forgive me for my sins and what I am about to do."

She picked up her alarm clock and set the alarm for midnight, knowing Wanda and Enoch would be sound asleep.

Sleep refused to come while her mind was so heavy with her thoughts. Wide awake, Gladys went over her life and wondered why she didn't follow God's way. She said aloud to the ceiling, "I would not be lying here in this bed waiting for the end if I had been a better sheep in God's flock."

When the alarm finally and inevitably went off, Gladys lifted herself upright on to the edge of the bed. Slowly, she transferred herself to the wheelchair just as she'd done with Nurse Hal watching her. She turned the wheels on the chair until she aimed herself around the end of the quilt. She rolled passed the rocking chairs and into the kitchen.

She opened a drawer and took out a box of matches. With the box in her lap, she wheeled back to the rockers and stopped to look around this little home she had barely taken the time to get to know.

Gladys slid the box out of its cover and picked up a wooden match. She struck its head on the box side's sandpaper strip. Carefully to keep the flame burning, she laid it on the window sill facing the porch. She picked up the bottom of cotton half curtain and pushed the thin white material into the flame. It ignited. Yellow and red flames licked up the curtain as if they were in a hurry to get this job done.

Gladys backed up the wheelchair so she could watch. When the flames heated the wooden window sill and ate into the wood, creating a red porous glow she was satisfied. Gladys turned around and rolled back behind the quilt. She calmly transferred herself into the bed and covered up.

With one arm over her eyes so she couldn't see the red flickers on the wall, she waited for what was to come as she heard the crackles and snaps of the fire eating away at the house. She smiled, complacent now that she knew she wasn't going to prison. This might be the very act of attrition that would keep Wanda and Enoch from being shunned in their new home. The fire would end it all here for her and serve as her punishment. This much she could do for herself and her family.

Loud crackling noises woke Wanda and Enoch. They

jumped out of bed in a bedroom much lighter than it should have been for the middle of the night. Wanda ran out on the porch and screamed her sister's name as she sank to her knees. The fiery heat made Wanda think of Hell. She prayed for the Lord to forgive her sister and hoped he was listening.

A lump grew in Wanda's throat as Gladys house was completely engulfed in fire. Wanda had not one bit of doubt that her sister set the fire. She searched for Gladys in the yard that was now all a glow, but she knew in her soul Gladys was burning right along with her house. Horrified about her sister's suffering, Wanda watched the crackling roar of the inferno and hoped that the end had come swiftly for her sister.

As proof that Gladys was not going easily, Wanda heard long, horrendously painful screams wailing from the middle of the inferno. The screams ceased when the roof fell in. Red sparks of fire shot above the house, caught on the breeze and sailed high into the sky.

Wanda gripped a porch post, stared as the wavering sparks moved as one toward Heaven. Convinced that she was seeing the spirit of her sister rising up, Wanda ask God to accept the soul of her tormented sister, Gladys Kraybill and make her heavenly stay more peaceful than her stay on earth had been.

Enoch knew it was too late to try to save Gladys the minute he saw the house in flames. He mounted one of the horses in the barn and raced to the phone shed to call the fire department. He wanted the fire put out before the sparks landed on his house.

Next he called the sheriff's office. Since he knew the sheriff was coming out in the morning, maybe he wouldn't want to bother if he knew Gladys had died.

Once the fire cooled off enough for investigators to hunt for the body, they recovered bits and pieces of the body to place in a pine box.

The funeral was like any other Amish funeral with the visitation in Enoch and Wanda's living room. People from the Plain community passed by the unopened coffin, expressing their condolences to Enoch and Wanda for the loss of Wanda's sister even though they didn't know her.

Outside, they paused to stare at the pile of smoking rubble and feel sorry for the poor woman who died so horribly at the hands of the arsonist. Now all the Plain community could think about was whose building would be next and would someone else die by fire?

The next morning, everyone came back for the funeral. They parked their buggies in line on the road ready to drive to the cemetery.

After a brief service in the Bruner living room, everyone filed out and headed for their buggies. At the grave site, Bishop Bontrager led the Lord's Prayer and a hymn. He ended the service by reading a verse from Job chapter three verse seventeen. "There the wicked cease from troubling; And there the weary are at rest."

The verse seemed like a strange one to quote at the funeral of an ailing woman that was burnt alive in her home by a madman. Such an invalid was the poor woman that she was unable to save herself.

After the funeral luncheon in the Bruner home, men mingled around outside. Some of the elders gathered out of the wind by the barn. Among themselves, it was whispered how worried they were about what the coming days would bring. Their prophecy of someone dying in one of the fires had come true. And wasn't that the oddest verse Bishop Bontrager read at the graveside? What did he mean to say with that verse?

It was Rudy Briskey that came up with the answer. The bishop surely meant with this death the arsonist might cease to set another fire. Now that he'd be branded a killer, he'd move on before he got caught.

That sounded logical to the other men. They passed this reasoning on to the rest of congregation. Everyone prayed the bishop was right, and it would be so that the arsonist wouldn't bother Plain people again. They agreed that Gladys Kraybill was the weary at rest as mentioned in the Job verse by Bishop Bontrager. They prayed that now she was at peace in the hands of the Lord.

Amish Recipes

Aunt Tootie's Favorite

Amish Chicken Corn Soup

This 4 quarts of soup serves 16 people. Large amounts of this soup would be used at many of the Amish gatherings such as craft shows, fairs, benefits or barn raisings to name a few events.

Prep 15 minutes   Cooking Time 40 minutes

12 cups water
2 pounds boneless skinless chicken breast, cubed
1 cup chopped onion
1 cup chopped celery
1 cup shredded carrots
3 chicken bouillon cubes
2 cans (14 ¾ oz) cream style corn.
2 cups uncooked egg noodles
¼ cup butter
1 teaspoon salt
¼ teaspoon pepper

In Dutch oven, combine water, chicken, onion, celery, carrots and bouillon cubes. Slowly bring to a boil. Reduce heat and simmer uncovered for thirty minutes or until chicken is no longer pink and vegetables are tender. Stir in corn, noodles and butter. Cook 10 minutes or until noodles are tender. Season with salt and pepper.

Emma Lapp's Favorite
Amish Tomato Gravy

1 quart canned, peeled, chopped tomatoes
3 tablespoon flour
2 to 3 tablespoon water
4 tablespoon brown sugar

Heat tomatoes to boiling point. Meanwhile, in separate boil stir together flour and water. Mix until smooth. Stir tomatoes while pouring flour mixture and brown sugar in. Cook until thick.

Serve over fried potatoes or Mac and Cheese.

Can add salt to taste. Amish canned tomatoes would have salt in it. A tablespoon or two of butter and parsley.

Hal's favorite salad

Amish Broccoli Salad

1 head of broccoli, chopped
1 head of cauliflower, chopped
1 cup mayonnaise
1 cup sour cream
½ cup sugar
½ teaspoon salt
½ pound bacon, fried and scrambled
1 cup shredded Cheddar cheese

Mix all together and chill.

Nora's favorite green bean dish

Pennsylvania Dutch Style Green Beans

3 strips bacon, cut up
1 small onion, cut up
2 teaspoons cornstarch
¼ teaspoon salt
¼ teaspoon dry mustard
1 tablespoon brown sugar
1 tablespoon vinegar
1 quart jar green beans

Fry bacon until crisp. Drain fat except for 1 tablespoon. Add onion and brown. Stir in cornstarch, salt, dry mustard and ½ liquid from green beans. Stir all together until mixture comes to a boil. Blend in brown sugar and vinegar. Add green beans and mix.

Spoon in greased casserole dish and put in 350 degree oven until throughly heated. This can be prepared the day before and served hot or cold.

Serves 6

Jim's Favorite Cake

Raw Apple Cake

1 ½ cups sugar
½ cup shortening
2 eggs
1 teaspoon vanilla
2 ½ cup flour
1 ½ teaspoon salt
3 cups chopped apples

Crumb Topping
8 tablespoon brown sugar
4 tablespoon flour
4 tablespoon butter

In bowl, cream together the sugar, shortening, eggs and vanilla. Add half of the 2 ½ cups of flour, soda and salt. Stir well, add chopped apples, then the rest of the dry ingredients. Fold in well. Pour in 9 x 13 greased and floured pan.

For topping, combine brown sugar, flour and butter. Mix until crumbly and sprinkle over cake batter. Bake for 50 minutes in 350 degree oven. Good served warm with ice cream.

Amish Molasses Pie

This Amish pie is made with molasses as the filling. Because it is so sweet the pie attracts flies which has to shooed away. That is why the Amish call it Shoo Fly Pie.

Shoo Fly Pie

One 9 inch pie crust

For filling

1 cup flour
2/3 cups brown sugar
1 tablespoon vegetable shortening
1 large egg
1 teaspoon baking soda
¾ cup boiling water

Mix together first three ingredients until shortening is integrated. Reserve ½ cup of mixture for later. Add molasses, egg and baking soda. Mix then add water and mix, scraping down the sides and bottom of the bowl. Pour filling in the pie crust and scattered the reserved ½ cup over the filling.

Bake 375 degrees for 18 minutes and lower temperature to 350 degrees for 18 to 20 minutes until crust is golden and center is only a bit wobbly. Cool pie on a rack. Serve with whip cream or ice cream.

Amish Taffy

2 cups sugar
1 cup molasses
¼ cup water
2 teaspoons white vinegar
2 tablespoon butter
½ teaspoon baking soda

Lightly grease baking sheet.

Bring sugar, molasses, water and vinegar to a boil in pan over medium heat. Cook and stir until sugar reaches hard boil stage at 250 to 255 degrees.

Test by dropping small amount of syrup into cold water to form a rigid ball.

Remove from heat and stir in butter and baking soda. Pour onto baking sheet. Allow to cool enough to handle at least ten to fifteen minutes.

Grease hands. Fold taffy in half then pull to double its original length. Continue folding and pulling until the taffy turns golden brown in about 15 to 20 minutes. It will be too stiff to pull anymore.

Cut taffy in bite size pieces and wrap in wax paper. Store in airtight container. Makes 30 pieces.

Amish Bumbleberry Pie

Not long ago we attended a livestock auction and stayed to watch the Amish baked goods and small animals and birds sell. One of the pies auctioned was a bumbleberry pie. Of course, I think I know every kind of berry there is since I raise most of them.

Very curious, I asked the Amish waitress at the salebarn cafe what a bumbleberry looked like.

The young woman gave me a puzzled looked. "You mean bumbleberry pie?"

"Yes, one sold at the auction just now."

"I'm not sure what's in that pie," the waitress said.

"Does bumbleberry mean something in Pennsylvania Dutch?" I asked.

"Nah," she said and left to wait on another customer.

I wasn't about to let this go so I came home and googled bumbleberry. It turned out to be a combination of odd and end berries that have been frozen in small batches near the end of the crops. Black ones are thrown into one pie to get a dark pie using black raspberries, blackberries and blueberries. Or use strawberries, rhubarb, red raspberries and apples for a red pie.

Mix together enough of your odd and end berries (fresh and frozen) to fill the crust of a nine inch pie, sugar to taste and use flour or cornstarch to thicken. Bake for 45 minutes at 350 degrees or until juice bubbles through the lattice crust on top.

Amish Food for a Barn Raising

This list of food was found in an old handwritten recipe book from Amish days gone by.

115 lemon pies
500 doughnuts
15 large cakes
3 gallon applesauce
3 gallon rice pudding
3 gallon cornstarch pudding
16 chickens
2 hams
50 pounds roast beef
300 light rolls
16 loaves of homemade bread
red beet pickles and pickled eggs
cucumber pickles
6 pounds dried prunes, stewed
1 large crock stewed raisins
5 gallon jar white potatoes
5 gallon jar sweet potatoes

This is enough food for 175 men.

About the Author

Fay Risner lives with her husband on a central Iowa acreage along with their chickens, rabbits, goats and cats. A former Certified Nurse Aide at the Keystone Nursing Care Center in Keystone, Iowa, she now divides her time between writing books, working in her flower beds and the garden and going fishing with her husband in their boat.

Fay writes books in various genre – historical mystery series, western series, Amish series set in southern Iowa and two books for Caregivers about Alzheimer's and some novellas.

She uses 12 font print in her books and 14 font print for her novellas to make them reader friendly. Her books have a mid western Iowa and small town flavor. She pulls the readers into her stories, making it hard for them to put a book down until the reader sees how the story ends. Readers say the characters are fun to get to know and often humorous enough to cause the readers to laugh out loud. The books leave the readers wanting a sequel or a series so they can read about the characters again.